Bridging Worlds:

THE LEGACY OF ARTISAN REALMS

ODECE BROOKS

PROLOGUE

Jason Beam, a visionary tech entrepreneur, and Kimberly Walker, an artist passionate about cultural heritage, founded "Artisan Realms." This platform was their dream—to connect the world with the blend of artisan crafts through the lens of technology.

Their journey was one of love, innovation, and the fusion of seemingly disparate worlds. Together, they created a space where art and digital marketplace converged, offering artisans a global stage.

The birth of their son, O'Brian, introduced a new hope to their legacy. A child of remarkable intellect and curiosity, he was the perfect blend of his parents' worlds. But fate had its own design. The tragic loss of Jason and Kimberly in a plane crash left "Artisan Realms" and young O'Brian at a crossroads.

The prologue of this story is a reflection on the indomitable spirit of dreams and the legacy of those who dare to envision a connected world. As O'Brian steps forward to lead "Artisan Realms," he carries the torch of his parents' dreams, facing the future with resilience and the promise of innovation.

This narrative sets the stage for a journey of memory, growth, and the enduring impact of a vision that seeks to bridge the gap between tradition and technology. It is a tale of legacy, not just of what is left behind, but of what is yet to be built— a legacy that shines brightly into the future, guiding the path of "Artisan Realms" and its young leader, O'Brian.

ISBN: 978-1-7381872-4-9
Odece Brooks
odecebrooks@gmail.com
www.odece.icu/books
Kingston, Jamaica

CHAPTER 1

DREAMS IN KINGSTON

Kingston's morning sun spilled golden light across the city, weaving through the bustling streets and touching the vibrant stalls of the local markets. In the heart of this lively city lived Jason Beam, 19-year-old university prodigy with eyes full of dreams bigger than the island of Jamaica itself.

Jason's day began like any other, with the aromatic scent of Blue Mountain coffee wafting through the modest, middle-class home he shared with his family. The Beams were well-respected in their community—hardworking, with a strong sense of pride in their Jamaican heritage. His father, a mechanic, and his mother, a school teacher, had instilled in Jason and his younger sister, Leah, the value of education and the importance of pursuing their passions.

Despite the love and laughter that filled their home, Jason often found himself gazing out beyond the cityscape, dreaming of a future that stretched far across the ocean to Canada. He harbored ambitions of becoming a tech entrepreneur, inspired by stories of innovation and success that seemed worlds away from the rhythm and routine of Kingston life.

Jason's passion for technology was more than just a dream; it was a plan in motion. He spent countless hours learning coding and business management online, while pursuing a bachelors in computer science. His laptop, a constant companion amid the backdrop of reggae music and the lively chatter of his family. Yet, the more he learned, the more he realized the limitations he faced in his current environment. Resources were scarce, opportunities limited, and the tech industry in Jamaica was still in its infancy.

As he walked through the streets of Kingston on his way to school, Jason couldn't help but feel a mix of love and frustration. He adored his country, with its rich culture, warm people, and breathtaking landscapes, but he also yearned for the opportunities that seemed just out of reach. The contrast between his everyday life and his dreams was stark, yet it fueled his determination.

Today, however, was not just another day. It marked the beginning of his final year of college, a reminder that his dreams of moving to Canada and becoming a tech entrepreneur were closer than ever. As he navigated through the crowded campus, greeted by friends and professors alike, Jason felt a surge of anticipation.

But even as he focused on his studies and plans, Jason couldn't shake off a feeling of restlessness. There was a part of him that wondered what life had in store, what unexpected turns awaited just around the corner. Little did he know, his world was about to change in ways he could never have imagined, starting with an encounter on the beaches of Jamaica that would turn his well-laid plans on their head.

CHAPTER 2

THE FABRIC OF FAMILY

The Beam household was alive with activity as the day wound down, the setting sun casting long shadows across the streets of Kingston. Inside, the aroma of dinner filled the air, a blend of spices and flavors that was distinctly Jamaican. Jason's mother, Marlene, was the undisputed queen of the kitchen, her cooking was a loving testament to the island's culinary heritage.

Jason sat at the worn, wooden dining table, his laptop open in front of him, but his attention was on his mother. He watched her move with practiced ease, adding ingredients to the pot on the stove, her movements a dance perfected through years of experience.

"Whatcha working on, Jason?" Marlene asked without turning, her tone casual but laced with genuine interest. "Just some coding, Mom. Trying to get ahead before final year officially starts," Jason replied, minimizing a window filled with lines of code to give her his full attention.

Marlene turned, wiping her hands on her apron, her face breaking into a proud smile. "You're going to do great things, mi son. Just remember, wherever you go, bring a piece of Jamaica with you."

Jason smiled, a warmth spreading through him at her words. "Always, Mom. Jamaica is in my heart, no matter where I am."

As they sat down to eat, Jason's father, David, and his sister, Leah, joined. After pecking his wife on the cheek, David found his place at the head of the table. The dinner table was a vibrant display of Jamaican cuisine—jerk chicken, rice and peas, and fried plantain. Dinner was more than a meal, it was a ritual, a time for the family to come together, share stories, and enjoy the fruits of their labor.

The conversation flowed easily, ranging from Leah's upcoming school project on Jamaican heroes to David's recounting of a particularly challenging day at the garage. Jason listened and chimed in, but his thoughts never strayed far from his dreams. He wondered, with a pang of longing, if his family truly understood the depth of his ambition, the drive that pushed him to envision a life beyond the island's shores.

After dinner, Jason helped clear the table, feeling a mix of gratitude and restlessness, before retreating to his room—a small, modest space he had made his own. Posters of tech icons and quotes about innovation adorned the walls, a stark contrast to the rest of the house's warm, traditional decor. Each poster was a silent testament to his aspirations, a beacon of hope in his secluded sanctuary.

He sat at his desk, headphones on, losing himself in the world of programming. The challenges he faced were complex, but they invigorated him, providing a sense of purpose and a thrilling escape from reality. Yet, even as he worked, his mind wandered to Canada and the possibilities that lay in its bustling tech scene. He imagined walking through a city filled with people from all corners of the world, sharing ideas, and building the future. The thought filled him with both excitement and fear—a thrilling anticipation of what could be, and a gnawing anxiety about the unknown.

But his dreams were tempered by reality. The path to Canada, to becoming a tech entrepreneur, was fraught with obstacles —financial, bureaucratic, and personal. Jason knew the journey would require more than just skill and passion; it would demand resilience, a quality he was determined to prove he possessed. He felt a surge of determination mixed with doubt, a cocktail of emotions that kept him awake at night and driven during the day.

As the night deepened, Jason finally closed his laptop, the code on the screen a testament to his dedication. He lay in bed, gazing out the window at the stars, the constellations mapping out his distant dreams. In the stillness of the night, he made a silent vow to himself and to the island that had raised him. He would succeed, not just for himself, but for his family, for Jamaica. He would build bridges, not just in the digital world, but between his past and his future.

A wave of emotion washed over him—hope, determination, and a touch of fear. The dreams of one young man in Kingston were set against the vast panorama of the world, a poignant reminder that even the most ambitious journeys begin with a single step, taken with hope and heart. Jason's heart beat with the rhythm of his aspirations, each thump a promise to his homeland and to himself. As he drifted into sleep, he clung to the belief that his dreams were within reach, fueled by the love and resilience that had always guided him.

CHAPTER 3

A STRANGER IN PARADISE

The warmth of the Jamaican sun was a stark contrast to the cool, crisp air Kimberly Walker had left behind in Toronto. As she stepped off the plane and onto the tarmac at Norman Manley International Airport, a rush of excitement mixed with a hint of nervousness flowed through her. Jamaica was a world away from the bustling streets and modern skyline of her hometown, a fact that was immediately apparent in the vibrant colors, lush landscapes, and the melodic rhythm of Patois that filled the air around her.

Kimberly was no stranger to travel, having explored various corners of the globe, but Jamaica held a special allure. It wasn't just the promise of sandy beaches and crystal-clear waters that had drawn her here; it was the desire to reconnect with an old college friend, Tanya, who had moved back to Jamaica after graduation. The trip was a spontaneous decision, a break from her routine job in digital marketing, and an opportunity to experience life on the island firsthand.

As she navigated through the bustling airport, Kimberly's thoughts drifted to what lay ahead. Tanya had promised a genuine Jamaican experience, far removed from the tourist traps and all-inclusive resorts. Kimberly was eager to dive into the culture, the food, the music, and most importantly, the people who called this island home.

Her first impressions did not disappoint. The drive from Montego Bay to Kingston revealed a blend of life that was both exhilarating and overwhelming. The streets were alive with activity, from street vendors selling their wares—jerk chicken to mangoes—to the lively beats of reggae music emanating from passing cars. The vibrant energy of the city was palpable, each scene a snapshot of a place rich with culture.

Upon arriving in Kingston, Kimberly was greeted by Tanya with a warm embrace. "Welcome to Jamrock, Kim!" Tanya exclaimed, her excitement infectious. "You're going to love it here!"

The first few days were a whirlwind of activity. Tanya introduced Kimberly to the real Jamaica, taking her to local markets, hidden beaches, and vibrant dance parties. They indulged in the island's culinary delights, from ackee and saltfish to spicy jerk pork, each dish a revelation to Kimberly's palate.

Yet, for all the beauty and warmth she encountered, Kimberly couldn't shake a feeling of being an outsider. The cultural differences were stark, and she found herself navigating unfamiliar social norms and expectations. It was both thrilling and challenging, a constant balancing act between embracing the new and holding onto the familiar.

One afternoon, as Kimberly sat on a secluded beach, watching the waves crash against the shore, she reflected on her journey so far. Jamaica was beautiful, complex, and full of contrasts, much like her own life. She realized that this trip was more than just a vacation; it was a journey of discovery, not just of Jamaica but of herself.

Little did she know, her adventure was about to take an unexpected turn. A chance encounter on this very beach would challenge her perceptions, push her out of her comfort zone, and ultimately, lead her to a connection that would change her life forever.

CHAPTER 4

WHEN PATHS CROSS

Today was Jason' day off from his part time gig and seeing as school was out for summer break, he too decided to take a break from the relentless pursuit of his dreams, a rare pause in his busy life to recharge and find inspiration. He decided to spend it at one of his favorite spots, a secluded beach not far from the hustle and bustle of the city but worlds away in terms of peace and tranquility.

Kimberly, seeking a quiet moment away from the whirlwind of her cultural immersion, found herself drawn to the same secluded beach. With her friend Tanya tied up with family obligations, Kimberly ventured out alone, eager to soak in the serene beauty of the Jamaican coastline.

Their paths crossed on a narrow stretch of sand, where the beach curved gently into a hidden cove. Jason, lost in thought, nearly bumped into Kimberly as she stood gazing out at the sea, her eyes reflecting the vastness before her. "Sorry, didn't see you there," Jason apologized, stepping back to give her space.

Kimberly turned, surprised by the sudden interruption to her solitude. "It's okay," she replied, her tone polite but guarded. "I was just... taking it all in."

An awkward silence fell between them as they looked on in quiet awe of each other, the easy rhythm of the waves filling the space. Kimberly looked away first, and Jason, sensing her discomfort, was about to move on when something made him pause. Perhaps it was the faraway look in her eyes or the way she seemed both present and miles away at the same time.

"You're not from around here, are you?" Jason asked, curiosity getting the better of him.

Kimberly smiled, a bit taken aback by his directness. "Is it that obvious?"

"A bit," Jason admitted with a chuckle. "I'm Jason, by the way."

"Kimberly," she said, returning the smile.

They stood there for another moment, two strangers connected by the serendipity of a shared space, trying not to stare at each other. Jason, ever the ambassador for his beloved island, found himself wanting to show this beautiful outsider why Jamaica was more than just a tourist destination.

"First time in Jamaica?" Jason asked, leaning casually against a nearby palm tree.

"Yes," Kimberly replied, warming up to the conversation. "I'm here visiting a friend."

"What do you think of it so far?" Jason was genuinely interested. He loved hearing people's impressions of his home country but more than that, he was enjoying the sparkle in her eyes.

"It's beautiful, overwhelming, and... complex," Kimberly chose her words carefully, wanting to convey her respect and the depth of her experience without sounding superficial.

Jason nodded, understanding the sentiment. "It's a lot to take in. But the real beauty of Jamaica isn't just in the landscapes or the music. It's in the people, the culture, the spirit of resilience and joy that pervades everything."

Kimberly listened, intrigued by his perspective and a bit flushed by his intelligence. This wasn't the Jamaica she'd read about in travel brochures or online articles. This was something deeper, more authentic, with a smart ... handsome man

"Would you... I mean, if you're not busy, I could show you some of my favorite spots," Jason found himself offering. "Places you won't find in any guidebook."

Broken out of her reverie, Kimberly hesitated, aware of the usual warnings about strangers. Yet, looking at Jason, with his earnest expression, his kind eyes, and timid smile she felt a surprising surge of trust.

"That sounds amazing," she finally said. "I'd love that."

And so, they set off together, Jason leading the way. As they walked, the initial awkwardness faded, replaced by a budding curiosity about each other. For Jason, it was a chance to share the Jamaica he knew and loved. For Kimberly, it was an opportunity to see the island through the eyes of someone who called it home, and for both, a little... more.

Little did they know, this chance encounter would mark the beginning of a journey neither had anticipated. A journey that would challenge their perceptions, test their boundaries, and ultimately, intertwine their destinies in ways they could never have imagined.

CHAPTER 5

DISCOVERING NEW WORLDS

Jason led Kimberly away from the familiar paths trodden by tourists, into the heart of Jamaica's lush landscapes and vibrant communities. Their first stop was a small, family-owned café nestled in the mountains overlooking Kingston. Here, the air was cooler, and the coffee was rich with history and flavor.

"This place has the best Blue Mountain coffee you'll ever taste," Jason boasted, his pride in his country evident in his voice. Kimberly, intrigued by his enthusiasm, followed him inside. The café was cozy, filled with the aroma of freshly ground coffee beans and the sound of reggae music playing softly in the background.

As they sat down to enjoy their coffee, the conversation flowed effortlessly and the laughs were plenty. Jason talked about his dreams of becoming a tech entrepreneur, his desire to bring innovation from his exploration of Canada back to Jamaica, and his hope of creating opportunities for his community. Kimberly listened, fascinated by his ambition and the depth of his commitment to his home.

In turn, Kimberly shared her own experiences, her work in digital marketing, her passion for travel, and art. She spoke of the places she'd seen and the diversity of cultures she'd experienced, but also of the sense of disconnection that often accompanied her journeys. With Jason, she felt a different kind of connection, grounded in genuine interest and understanding.

After the café, Jason took Kimberly to a hidden beach he had discovered as a child. It was a place untouched by development, where the natural beauty of Jamaica was on full display. As they walked along the shore, fingers lightly grazing, their conversation deepened, touching on topics of culture, identity, and the complexities of navigating a globalized world

Kimberly was struck by the contrast between the Jamaica she had imagined and the one she was experiencing with Jason. It was a place of stunning natural beauty, yes, but also of rich cultural heritage, resilience, and a vibrant sense of community. She found herself seeing the island—and Jason— in a new, different light.

The day passed in a blur of new experiences and shared moments. They laughed, debated, and occasionally fell into comfortable silences, simply enjoying each other's company. As the sun began to set, painting the sky in hues of orange and pink, they found themselves at a local eatery, trying traditional Jamaican dishes at Jason's insistence.

"It's been an amazing day," Kimberly said, her voice sincere and dreamy. "Thank you for showing me your Jamaica." she said as she gazed into his gentle eyes.
Jason smiled, a sense of satisfaction filling him. "I'm glad you enjoyed it. There's so much more to see, though. Maybe we can do this again?"

The question hung in the air, charged with the possibility of more days like this one. Kimberly nodded, her smile matching his. "I'd like that."

As they parted ways, with promises to meet again soon, both felt a stirring of something new. It was too soon to define, but the connection between them was undeniable. For Jason, Kimberly was not just a holiday fling but someone he could envision being with for a lifetime. She represented a window to the world beyond Jamaica, a connection deeper than any he had experienced before, and he felt compelled to explore it. For Kimberly, Jason was a grounding presence, a reminder of the beauty and depth to be found in every place if only one took the time to look.

CHAPTER 6

REFLECTIONS AND REALIZATIONS

After parting ways with Kimberly, Jason found himself walking home under the starlit sky, his mind replaying moments from the day. Each laugh shared, every serious discussion, and the way her eyes lit up in wonder at the sights of his Jamaica filled him with a sense of fulfillment he hadn't known he was missing. It was a day unlike any other, and as he lay in bed later, thoughts of Kimberly invaded his dreams, blending with his aspirations and hopes for the future, and he drifted off to sleep with a genuine smile.

Meanwhile, Kimberly returned to her temporary home, her mind swirling with the day's experiences. Jason had shown her a side of Jamaica that was both beautiful and real, far removed from the glossy images of travel blogs. But it was not just the island that had captivated her; it was Jason himself. His passion for his country, his dreams of making a difference, and the easy way he shared his world with her had left her in amazement. As she drifted off to sleep, she wondered about the possibilities that lay ahead, both for her journey in Jamaica and the unexpected connection she had found with Jason.That night dreams of a future with a mysteriously familiar man plagued her sleep.

The following day, Jason was back to his routine, but the spark of something new lingered in his thoughts. He found himself reaching out to Kimberly, suggesting another meet-up under the guise of continuing to show her the "real" Jamaica. Deep down, he knew it was more than just hospitality driving him; it was a desire to see her pretty hazel eyes again, to explore the connection that had begun to form between them.

Kimberly, on her end, welcomed Jason's message with a mix of excitement and trepidation. She had traveled enough to know that holiday romances were often fleeting, built on the novelty of new experiences rather than lasting compatibility. Yet, something about Jason felt different, real, grounded in shared values and genuine rapport rather than mere circumstance.

Their next meeting was filled with a palpable sense of anticipation. They ventured further into the heart of the island, exploring cultural landmarks and engaging in deep conversations about their dreams, fears, and the challenges they faced in their respective pursuits. With each shared experience, the initial spark between them grew into a steady flame, lighting up the possibility of something more.

However, as their connection deepened, so too did the realization of the obstacles that lay ahead. Jason was acutely aware of the differences in their lives and backgrounds. Kimberly was a visitor to his country, with a life and career she had to return to in Canada. And while he harbored dreams of leaving Jamaica to pursue his ambitions, he had too much unfinished business in Jamaica to leave now. He knew the path would be fraught with challenges, not least of which was the potential distance between them.

For Kimberly, the thought of leaving Jamaica now carried a bittersweet edge. What had started as a simple vacation had evolved into a journey of self-discovery, with Jason playing a central role. The prospect of returning to her life in Canada, leaving behind the connection they had built, filled her with a sense of unease.

CHAPTER 7

THE TIDE OF TRADITION

The rhythm of life in Kingston, with its vibrant culture and deeply rooted traditions, had always been a source of pride for Jason. Yet, as he introduced Kimberly to more of his life, including friends and family, the differences between their worlds became more pronounced. It wasn't just the cultural nuances that stood out; it was the expectations and assumptions made by others about their long distance relationship.

At a family gathering to celebrate Jason's achievement, he was awarded the "Science and Technology Youth Award." Kimberly was introduced to Jason's extended family. The couple found themselves navigating a sea of questions and subtle judgments. Jason's relatives were warm and welcoming but also curious and sometimes too direct in their inquiries about Kimberly's background, intentions, and understanding of Jamaican culture.

Kimberly, for her part, felt the weight of expectation to fit into a world that was both beautiful and complex. She was keen to show her respect and appreciation for the culture but found herself struggling to bridge the gap between being a visitor and being seen as a part of Jason's life. The experience was eye-opening, highlighting the challenges of blending two distinct cultures and the pressure to conform to traditional expectations.

Meanwhile, Jason faced his own internal conflict. He was torn between his desire to share his world with Kimberly and the protective instinct to shield her from the scrutiny and expectations of his community. He understood that his relationship with Kimberly might be viewed with skepticism, a reflection of broader concerns about cultural preservation and the influences of outsiders.

The evening, though filled with laughter and music, left Jason and Kimberly with much to ponder. On their way home, they discussed their feelings and the reactions they had encountered. It was a difficult conversation, one that exposed their vulnerabilities and the uncertainty of navigating a relationship that crossed cultural lines.
"I just want them to see you the way I do," Jason admitted, his voice tinged with frustration. "But I also understand where they're coming from. It's complicated."

Kimberly nodded, her mind racing with thoughts of her own place within Jason's world. "I get it, Jason. I really do. And I want to learn, to understand. But I also realize it's not something that can happen overnight. It's going to take time, for both of us."

The moment was a turning point, a realization that their journey together would require more than just mutual affection. It would demand patience, empathy, and a willingness to confront and overcome the barriers that stood in their way.

As they continued to talk, laying bare their fears and hopes, they found solace in their shared commitment to facing these challenges together. It was a testament to the strength of their connection, a bond that was being tested but also fortified through adversity.

CHAPTER 8

DREAMS INTERWOVEN

The morning after the family gathering, Jason and Kimberly met at a quiet café, a place that had become their refuge for honest conversations and planning their future. The air was thick with the scent of coffee and the undercurrent of their recent realization about the complexities of their relationship.

Kimberly initiated the conversation, her voice steady but filled with emotion. "I've been thinking a lot about what happened last night, about how we can move forward. I know we come from different worlds, but I believe in us, Jason. I believe in what we have been building."

Jason reached across the table, taking her hand in his. "I do too, Kimberly. It hasn't been easy, but I'm willing to do whatever it takes. We'll figure this out together like we've been doing."

As they delved into their aspirations and fears, Jason shared his dream of starting a tech company in Jamaica, aiming to create opportunities and foster growth in his homeland. He mentioned that he would use the money and exposure from the "Science and Technology Youth Award" to help start the company. Kimberly listened, her admiration for Jason deepening. She expressed her own ambitions in digital marketing and her desire to support Jason's goals, hinting at a significant decision she had been contemplating.

"The more I think about our dreams and what we want to achieve, the more I realize that being close to each other, supporting each other in person, is crucial," Kimberly said, her resolve clear. "That's why I've decided to temporarily move to Jamaica to start this new venture with you. It's a big step, but it feels right. It's not just about being physically together; it's about fully investing in our shared future, in this vision we have."

Jason was taken aback, overwhelmed by her commitment. "Kimberly, are you sure? This is a huge step."
"I am," she affirmed. "I believe in us, in this plan. It's the chance to blend our professional interests and really make a difference. And while we're doing that, we'll be learning and growing together, navigating the challenges of a cross-cultural relationship head-on."

This decision set the stage for the next chapter of their lives. They began to outline a detailed plan, leveraging Kimberly's expertise in digital marketing for Jason's tech company, and discussing the logistics of her move. They talked about the cultural exchanges they would experience, the professional challenges they would face, and the impact they hoped to have on Jamaica's growth.

Kimberly's move to Jamaica represented not just a physical shift but a deepening of their partnership. It was a testament to their determination to overcome obstacles, blending their dreams and cultures into a shared future filled with promise and potential.

CHAPTER 9

BRIDGING WORLDS

In their journey to blend their unique professional skills and rich cultural backgrounds into a shared dream, Jason and Kimberly faced a big challenge. They had a clear and exciting vision: to start their tech company in Jamaica that would bring new ideas to life and create jobs for local people. Kimberly knew a lot about marketing, and Jason had big dreams, the tech skills, the award funds, a small inheritance, but convincing other people to believe in their vision was like trying to climb the Blue Mountains.

The doubts from potential investors and people in the community were deep. Some wondered if Jason, with his strong ties to Jamaica, relatively limited experience, and Kimberly, who knew the world beyond its shores, could really work together in business as well as they did in life. They had to show everyone that their partnership was not just good for them but could be powerful and successful in the business world too.

So, Jason and Kimberly came up with a bold plan. They decided to attend a forum for the community, a special event where they could share their business idea. This event would be more than just a regular presentation. It would be a chance for them to show how their different backgrounds and youth were actually strengths, and how together they could bring something new and good to the local economy.

Night after night, they worked hard to get ready for this event. Their home turned into a workshop of ideas. They looked at every detail of their business plan, guessing the questions people might ask and finding the best answers. They practiced how to explain their ideas clearly and excitingly, wanting to show everyone the bright future they could create together.

Their preparation was a mix of careful planning and creative thinking. They didn't want to just talk about their business; they wanted to tell a story. A story about how two people from different worlds could come together and make something amazing. They were determined to change doubts into support, to show that their unique partnership was not just special but could really make a difference, bridge worlds.

CHAPTER 10

A UNIFIED VISION

The day of the forum arrived, and the room was filled with local entrepreneurs, potential investors, and members of the tech community. The air buzzed with anticipation and skepticism, a mix that fueled Jason and Kimberly's resolve.

Jason took the lead, sharing his journey, his passion for technology, and his vision for how his startup could change the face of tech in Jamaica. He spoke with conviction, his belief in his dream palpable in every word.

Kimberly followed, presenting their marketing strategy, showcasing how they planned to leverage digital platforms to reach a global audience while maintaining a strong local presence. She highlighted successful case studies and drew parallels to their venture, emphasizing the unique blend of cultures and perspectives that made their approach innovative.

As they answered questions from the audience, their synergy was evident. They addressed concerns with honesty and demonstrated a deep understanding of both the challenges and opportunities their venture faced. Slowly, the room's skepticism gave way to interest and then to enthusiasm. The community's support began to solidify around them, with offers of mentorship, investment, and collaboration.

By the end of the forum, Jason and Kimberly had not only convinced others of the viability of their venture but had also strengthened their own belief in the power of their partnership. They had faced a significant challenge and emerged stronger, their vision for the future clearer and more attainable than ever.

CHAPTER 11

FOUNDATIONS AND FRICTIONS

Riding the wave of support from the community forum, Jason and Kimberly began to lay the groundwork for their startup. Their days were filled with meetings with potential investors, brainstorming sessions, and planning the logistics of turning their vision into reality. The excitement of these initial steps was palpable, fueling their determination and passion for the project.

However, as they delved deeper into the intricacies of building a business together, the complexities of their professional and personal relationship began to surface. The blending of their different backgrounds and skill sets, while a strength, also introduced challenges. Decision-making became a test of compromise and compassion, as each brought their own perspectives and priorities to the table.

Jason, deeply rooted in his Jamaican identity and understanding of the local market, sometimes found Kimberly's international approach too detached from the realities on the ground. Conversely, Kimberly, with her experience in digital marketing and global trends, occasionally felt that Jason's focus was too narrow, potentially limiting their startup's reach and impact.

One afternoon, a heated discussion over the direction of their marketing strategy brought these tensions to a head. Jason argued for a campaign that highlighted the startup's contributions to local development, emphasizing its roots in Jamaican culture and community. Kimberly, while supportive of this focus, pushed for a broader appeal, aiming to attract international investors and a global audience.

The argument, though resolved with a compromise to incorporate both local and international elements into their strategy, was a sobering reminder of the challenges they faced. It underscored the need for clear communication and mutual respect for each other's expertise and perspectives.

In the aftermath, Jason and Kimberly took a step back to reassess their approach to working together. They agreed on setting clearer boundaries between their personal and professional lives and committed to regular check-ins to address any issues or concerns openly and constructively.

This episode of friction and resolution served as a crucial learning experience, strengthening their partnership. It highlighted the importance of balance—between their individual identities and their shared goals, between their commitment to their community and their aspirations for global reach.

CHAPTER 12

LAUNCHING DREAMS

The day of the launch arrived with a mixture of excitement and nerves. Jason and Kimberly's startup, a platform designed to connect local Jamaican artisans with global markets, was ready to be introduced to the world. The event was set in a beautifully restored warehouse in downtown Kingston, transformed into a vibrant space that reflected the spirit of their venture—innovative, community-focused, and deeply rooted in Jamaican culture.

As guests began to arrive, including local entrepreneurs, international investors, and members of the press, Jason and Kimberly worked the room, their chemistry and shared vision evident to all. The air buzzed with conversations about the potential of their platform to change lives, offering local artisans a global audience for their crafts while promoting sustainable, community-driven economic growth.

When it came time to present, Jason took the stage first, sharing the story of their startup's genesis—from a simple conversation on a secluded beach to the dynamic platform it had become. His voice was steady, filled with passion and pride, not just in their business but in the potential it had to make a real difference.

Kimberly followed, delving into some basic aspects of the platform and the marketing strategy that would propel it onto the global stage. Her presentation was polished and professional, yet it also conveyed a deep sense of commitment to their shared vision and the community that had inspired it.

The launch was more than just the unveiling of a new tech venture; it was a celebration of partnership, perseverance, and the power of bridging worlds. The feedback from attendees was overwhelmingly positive, with many expressing excitement about the platform's potential impact and eagerness to see how it would evolve.

As the evening wound down, Jason and Kimberly found a quiet moment to reflect on the journey that had brought them to this point. They talked about the challenges they had faced, the compromises they had made, and the growth they had experienced, both individually and together.

"This is just the beginning," Jason said, looking out at the guests mingling and exploring the platform through demo stations. "We've got a lot of work ahead of us, but after everything we've been through, I know we can handle it. Together."

Kimberly nodded, her hand finding Jason's. "Together," she echoed, her heart full of hope for their future. "We're making a difference, Jason. Not just for us, but for everyone we're hoping to help with this platform."

CHAPTER 13

NAVIGATING STORMY SEAS

The weeks following the launch had been a whirlwind of activity. Orders were coming in, artisans were engaging with the platform, and the buzz around their startup was growing. However, just as Jason and Kimberly began to feel they were finding their footing, a significant challenge emerged.

A major software bug was discovered, one that jeopardized the security of the platform's transactions. It was a critical issue that needed immediate attention, casting a shadow over their recent successes and putting their reputation at risk. The problem was complex, requiring not just a technical fix but a strategic approach to manage the fallout with their users and investors.

Jason took the lead on the technical side, working tirelessly with their development team to identify and fix the bug. His background in tech and his understanding of the platform's architecture were crucial in navigating this crisis. However, the stress of the situation weighed heavily on him, the fear of failure a constant presence.

Kimberly, recognizing the importance of transparent communication, took charge of managing the situation with their stakeholders. She crafted updates for their users, ensuring they were informed and reassured about the steps being taken to resolve the issue. Her experience in marketing and her skill in communication became invaluable assets, allowing them to maintain trust and mitigate the potential damage to their reputation.

As days turned into nights, and the problem persisted, the strain began to take its toll. The pressure to resolve the issue quickly was immense, testing the strength of Jason and Kimberly's relationship. They found themselves snapping at each other over minor issues, the tension a reflection of their underlying anxiety.

However, it was during one long night, as they sat side by side, poring over lines of code and drafting yet another update for their users, that they found their way back to each other. A shared look, a moment of understanding, reminded them of the bond they had formed, the challenges they had already overcome together.

"We'll get through this," Kimberly said, her voice soft but firm. "We always do." Jason looked at her, the weight of the past days evident in his eyes. "Together," he replied, the word a promise.

It took several more days of hard work, but eventually, the bug was fixed, and the platform was stronger for it. The crisis had been a stark reminder of the vulnerabilities inherent in their venture but also of the resilience they possessed as a team.

CHAPTER 14

STRENGTHENED BONDS

With the software bug firmly behind them, Jason and Kimberly took a moment to breathe and reflect. The crisis had been a harsh but valuable teacher. It taught them the importance of resilience, the strength of their partnership, and the need for a proactive approach to potential challenges. They emerged from the situation more united and determined, with a firmer grasp of the plan for the future of their startup.

The resolution of the crisis brought an unexpected surge in support from their community and users. Artisans on the platform expressed their gratitude for the transparency and swiftness of the response, while investors were impressed by the team's ability to handle adversity. This wave of positive feedback fueled a period of significant growth for the startup, attracting new artisans and customers, expanding their market reach, and solidifying their reputation as a trustworthy and innovative platform.

As the business began to stabilize and grow, Jason and Kimberly found themselves in a phase of strategic planning. They were keen to learn from their past mistakes, implementing robust testing and security measures to prevent similar issues. Moreover, they started exploring new technologies and partnerships that could enhance the platform's capabilities, making it more user-friendly and scalable.

Amidst this business expansion, their personal relationship also flourished. The challenges they faced together had deepened their understanding and appreciation for each other. They found a rhythm in balancing their work and personal lives, ensuring that their relationship remained a source of strength and joy amidst the demands of their growing venture.

One evening, as they walked along the same beach where their journey had begun, Jason turned to Kimberly with a sense of purpose in his eyes. "Remember when this was just an idea, a dream we were afraid to voice out loud?" he asked, his voice reflective.

Kimberly smiled, squeezing his hand. "I do. It feels like a lifetime ago. We've come so far, not just with the startup but with us."

Jason nodded, looking out at the horizon where the sky met the sea. "I've been thinking about the future, about our future. There's so much more we can do, so many more challenges we'll face. But I can't imagine doing it with anyone but you."

The conversation that followed was a mix of personal and professional dreams. They talked about expanding the platform to include more communities, exploring new markets, and perhaps one day, starting a foundation to support education and entrepreneurship in underserved areas. On a personal level, they discussed the possibility of making Jamaica their permanent home, building a life together where their love and work could intertwine.

CHAPTER 15

EXPANDING HORIZONS

The success of their startup had surpassed Jason and Kimberly's initial expectations. Buoyed by their recent triumph over adversity, and the solid foundation they had built, they were ready to take their venture to the next level. The expansion plan was ambitious, involving the introduction of new features to enhance the user experience and the exploration of new markets beyond Jamaica.

One of the innovative features they decided to introduce was a virtual marketplace, allowing artisans to showcase their products in a dynamic, interactive environment. This feature was designed to bridge the gap between traditional craftsmanship and digital convenience, offering customers a unique shopping experience that highlighted the stories behind the products and their creators.

Simultaneously, Jason and Kimberly began researching potential new markets. They recognized that the model they had developed could benefit artisans in other regions with rich cultural heritages but limited access to global markets. Identifying the right markets required careful consideration of various factors, including local infrastructure, the presence of artisan communities, and the legal and logistical challenges of international expansion.

As they embarked on this new phase, Jason and Kimberly faced a steep learning curve. They had to navigate the complexities of international business, from regulatory compliance to cultural sensitivities, ensuring that their expansion efforts were sustainable and respectful of the communities they aimed to serve.

Throughout this process, their partnership was tested in new ways. The pressure of making critical decisions for the future of their venture, coupled with the relentless pace of work, brought new stresses to their relationship. Yet they found strength in their shared vision and the deep trust they had built. Open communication and mutual support became their anchor, allowing them to navigate these challenges with grace and resilience.

Amidst the whirlwind of activity, Jason and Kimberly made it a point to step back and reflect on their journey. They organized a retreat for their team, a chance to celebrate their achievements, foster team spirit, and refocus on their mission. This retreat also served as a reminder of the importance of balance, encouraging everyone to take care of their well-being amidst the demands of scaling the business.

CHAPTER 16

THE STRENGTH OF TWO

The expansion was well underway, with new features rolling out and exploratory talks with artisans in other countries beginning to bear fruit. However, just as their professional lives were soaring, Jason and Kimberly encountered a personal challenge that brought a new level of complexity to their relationship.

Kimberly received news from home that her father was seriously ill. The distance between Jamaica and her hometown in Canada suddenly felt insurmountable. Torn between her commitments in Jamaica and her family back home, Kimberly was faced with a difficult decision. The situation was a stark reminder of the sacrifices involved in their entrepreneurial journey and the personal costs that often went unnoticed.

Jason, seeing the distress and conflict within Kimberly, immediately offered his unwavering support. He suggested that they take some time to go back to Canada to be with her family, reassuring her that their team could manage the startup in their absence. His primary concern was her well-being and that of her family, underscoring the depth of his commitment to her beyond their professional partnership. However, Kimberly insisted that he stay to guide the expansion as they were at a very crucial stage.

Kimberly's departure was a test of their trust and the systems they had put in place for their business. Jason found himself juggling multiple roles, striving to keep the momentum going while also dealing with his concern for Kimberly. The physical distance between them brought their own issues, but it also reinforced the strength of their communication and the solidity of their relationship.

During her time in Canada, Kimberly wrestled with feelings of guilt for leaving the startup at such a crucial time and worry over her father's health. Yet, through regular video calls and messages, Jason was a constant source of strength and encouragement, reminding her that she was where she needed to be, that he'd come to her if she said the word, and that their shared dreams were strong enough to withstand this challenge.

The situation brought to light the importance of balance and support in their relationship. It was a poignant reminder that their partnership was not just about building a business but about supporting each other through life's ups and downs.

After several weeks, Kimberly's father's condition stabilized, and she returned to Jamaica, her relief and gratitude evident. The reunion with Jason was sweet yet emotional, a testament to the bond they had forged through their shared experiences, both professional and personal.

In the aftermath, Jason and Kimberly always made sure they took steps to ensure that their startup was resilient, not just in the face of business challenges but also personal ones. They implemented strategies to maintain work-life balance, prioritize well-being, and foster a supportive team environment.

CHAPTER 17

A LEAP FORWARD

In the wake of overcoming personal challenges, Jason and Kimberly approached their work with renewed vigor and a deepened sense of partnership. The lessons learned during Kimberly's absence had not only strengthened their resolve but also enhanced their vision for the startup. It was during this period of focused ambition that an opportunity arose, one that could dramatically accelerate their growth and impact.

A major international retail chain, interested in diversifying its offerings with authentic, artisanal products, reached out to discuss a potential partnership. This opportunity represented everything Jason and Kimberly had been working towards: a chance to showcase the talent of local artisans on a global stage and to create a sustainable impact on the community.

Negotiations were intense and required a careful balance of assertiveness and compromise. Jason led the discussions, drawing on his deep understanding of the business and its mission, while Kimberly worked behind the scenes, crafting a marketing strategy that highlighted the unique value proposition of their platform.

The negotiations were evidence of their growth as entrepreneurs. They approached each meeting with a clear strategy, anticipating questions and objections, and presenting their case with confidence. The process was exhausting, filled with moments of doubt and tension, but Jason and Kimberly supported each other through it all, their relationship a source of strength and stability.

Finally, after weeks of back-and-forth, the deal was sealed. The partnership was more than just a business agreement; it was a validation of their hard work and a sign of the potential their startup had at making a real impact.. The news was met with celebration among their team and the artisan community they supported, a collective achievement that underscored the collaborative spirit of their venture.

To mark this milestone, they decided to throw a celebration at the office. Jason invited his mom Marlene, his dad David, and his sister Leah to join the festivities. The presence of his family added a personal touch to the festivities, which made Jason very happy to know that he could share such an accomplishment with the people nearest and dearest to him.

The partnership brought about a whirlwind of activity. Preparing for the scale-up required careful planning and execution. Jason and Kimberly worked tirelessly, coordinating with artisans, streamlining operations, and ensuring that the quality and authenticity of the products remained at the heart of their expansion.

Amidst this busy period, they also took time to reflect on the journey that had brought them here. They recognized that this milestone was just the beginning of a new chapter, one filled with potential but also new challenges. The scale of their operation had changed, and with it, the stakes became higher.

CHAPTER 18

SCALING WITH INTEGRITY

The success of the partnership brought about an exhilarating phase of growth for the startup. Orders were pouring in, the artisan community was expanding, and their team needed to grow to manage the increased workload. With growth came new challenges—maintaining the quality of the products, ensuring the well-being of their artisans, and preserving the startup's culture and values.

Jason and Kimberly found themselves at the helm of a rapidly evolving enterprise. The need for additional staff led to a hiring spree, and while this expansion was essential, it also introduced complexities in maintaining the close-knit, collaborative culture that had been a cornerstone of their success. They were determined to lead by example, fostering an environment that valued open communication, mutual respect, and a shared commitment to their mission.

One of the first tests of their expanded operation was managing the logistics of scaling production without compromising the quality or the ethical standards of their artisan products. Jason spearheaded initiatives to implement quality control systems and ethical sourcing guidelines, ensuring that growth did not come at the expense of their core principles.

Meanwhile, Kimberly focused on deepening the relationship with their new retail partner and the marketing efforts to support the expansion. She was mindful of the balance between meeting commercial targets and staying true to the core purpose of their brand, which highlighted the artisans' unique stories and the craftsmanship behind each product.

As they navigated these challenges, Jason and Kimberly also had to adapt their leadership styles. The transition from a startup to a more structured organization required a shift towards more strategic, long-term planning, while still maintaining the agility and innovative spirit that had driven their initial success. They invested in leadership training for themselves and their senior team members, recognizing that the growth of their company was intrinsically linked to their development as leaders.

The pressure of scaling also tested their personal relationship, as long hours and the constant barrage of decisions took their toll. However, they had learned from past challenges the importance of carving out time for each other, ensuring that their relationship was nurtured alongside their business. They instituted regular "off-the-grid" weekends, where they disconnected from work to focus on their personal connection, reaffirming their commitment to each other.

CHAPTER 19

RECOGNITION AND REFLECTION

As Jason and Kimberly's venture blossomed into a beacon of innovation and ethical entrepreneurship, it garnered widespread acclaim, drawing the eyes of not only a growing base of enthusiastic consumers and discerning investors but also pillars of the business world and champions of social change. Their platform, a fusion of cutting-edge technology and a deep commitment to ethical practices, began to set a new standard in the industry. This attention soon crystallized into a nomination for a prestigious award, one that celebrated trailblazers in sustainable business practices, marking a significant milestone in their journey.

The news of the nomination arrived as an unexpected token of recognition, a tactile affirmation that their venture was not just a business, but a movement making tangible impacts. As the date of the award ceremony drew near, Jason and Kimberly found themselves in a reflective mood, contemplating the road they had traveled. This introspection revealed a myriad of experiences — from the initial hurdles that seemed insurmountable to the exhilarating breakthroughs that propelled their project forward, from the personal evolutions they underwent to the professional strides they made, and most importantly, the visible benefits their work provided to the artisan community and the environment.

The award ceremony itself was nothing short of inspiring. Surrounded by like-minded entrepreneurs and innovators, all united by a common goal of contributing to a better, more sustainable world, Jason and Kimberly felt a profound sense of kinship with a global movement of positive change. When the moment came, and their startup was announced as the winner, the rush of emotions was overwhelming. It was a surreal validation of their years of dedication, hard work, and unwavering belief in their mission.

They took the stage hand in hand and as the announcer handed the mic to Jason he passed it to Kimberly with a proud smile. Kimberly delved into the importance of storytelling in their venture, explaining how sharing the narratives of artisans from around the world not only enriched their platform but also fostered a deeper connection among people across different cultures and continents. She spoke of the power of empathy and understanding in creating a more inclusive and interconnected world. Jason spoke with heartfelt sincerity about the core values that guided their journey — the importance of building a community focused, sustainable, and integrity driven business. He touched upon the challenges they faced, the lessons learned, and the victories won, emphasizing the collective effort of their team and the support of their community.

Their speeches, imbued with genuine emotion and insights, resonated deeply with the audience, leaving a lasting impression not just on those in the room but also echoing through social media and the press coverage, inspiring viewers everywhere.The recognition served as a catalyst, not just for Jason and Kimberly but for everyone who heard their story, to continue striving for innovation, sustainability, and social responsibility in business. The award was not just a trophy to display but a reminder and an encouragement to persist in their efforts to make the world a better place, one ethical business decision at a time.

CHAPTER 20

LOOKING TOWARDS THE HORIZON

Riding high on the wave of recognition and the platform it offered them, Jason and Kimberly found themselves filled with a newfound energy and purpose. They weren't just happy with what they had achieved; they were eager to push the boundaries even further. They dreamed of making their impact felt far and wide, of diving into the latest technologies to make their platform even better, and of building strong partnerships with others who shared their passion for supporting local artisans and promoting green, sustainable ways of doing business across the globe.

As they laid out the plans for this thrilling next step in their journey, Jason and Kimberly also realized the importance of keeping the spark alive in their personal relationship. They knew that their love and partnership built the foundation that everything else stood on. In an adventurous spirit, they decided to take a break—a sabbatical—to explore the world together. This wasn't just any break, but a time for them to step back, to soak in new experiences, to find fresh inspiration, and to dream even bigger dreams.

This sabbatical turned into a transformative experience for them. They traveled to breathtaking places, met people from all walks of life, and experienced the beauty of diverse cultures up close. Each new place they visited and every unique person they met added layers of inspiration and understanding to their vision. They saw the world through each other's eyes, learning more about each other and growing closer with each step they took.

This period of reflection and adventure reminded them of the reasons they started this journey together in the first place. Surrounded by the incredible beauty of nature and the richness of different cultures, Jason and Kimberly found new wells of inspiration. They returned from their travels not just rejuvenated, but with a deeper appreciation for each other's strengths, dreams, and the shared goals that brought them together. Their sabbatical was a vivid reminder of their mission, reigniting their passion and equipping them with new ideas and perspectives to bring back to their venture, ready to turn these new dreams into reality.

CHAPTER 21

NEW BEGINNINGS

As dawn broke, heralding their return and the beginning of a new chapter, Jason and Kimberly stood on the brink of an exciting transition. Their time away had not only rejuvenated their spirits but also sparked a flurry of innovative ideas and fresh perspectives. Eager to put these insights into practice, they were poised to lift their venture to new heights.

Gathering their team, who had skillfully steered the ship in their absence, was their first step. This gathering was more than just a meeting; it was a festive acknowledgment of the team's unwavering commitment, a collective brainstorming for the future, and an in-depth strategy session combined.

Fuelled by the inspiration from their travels, Jason and Kimberly unveiled a daring new initiative: to integrate virtual reality (VR) technology to craft immersive narratives that showcased the artisans' stories and their creations. This forward-thinking strategy aimed to bridge the gap between artisans and consumers, making the marketplace not just a transactional space but a rich environment of shared human experiences.

The proposal ignited a spark within the team, who were all too ready to dive into the project's technical and imaginative demands. This endeavor promised to distinguish their platform in the online world while doubling down on their dedication to ethical and sustainable entrepreneurship. It was an audacious move, signaling a collective effort to surpass their past accomplishments.

On a more personal note, Jason and Kimberly found themselves navigating the waters of new beginnings as well. The path they had traveled together had deepened, enriched by every hurdle and victory along the way. In light of this, they chose to reaffirm their bond, organizing a modest ceremony to honor their partnership, resilience, and mutual aspirations. This act was a reflection of their shared journey, a celebration of the strength and support they found in each other's love.

This spirit of renewal echoed throughout their business endeavors. As they embarked on the VR project, they also launched community outreach initiatives aimed at uplifting artisans, extending their reach beyond Jamaica to touch lives globally. Their ambition was growing, fueled by a relentless drive to affect meaningful change in the lives of individuals and communities alike.

CHAPTER 22

BRIDGING WORLDS

The development of the VR project, dubbed "Artisan Realms," was a journey filled with technical challenges, creative brainstorming, and strategic partnerships. Jason and Kimberly, along with their dedicated team, embarked on this venture with a clear objective: to revolutionize the way people connect with artisanal crafts, creating a virtual marketplace that offered immersive, interactive experiences.

To bring this vision to life, they collaborated with VR developers, cultural experts, and, most importantly, the artisans themselves. These collaborations were crucial in ensuring that the platform was not only technologically advanced but also culturally sensitive and authentic. The process was a learning experience for everyone involved, bridging the gap between traditional craftsmanship and cutting-edge technology.

As "Artisan Realms" neared completion, anticipation built among the startup team and the artisan community. The platform promised to offer users a unique insight into the artisans' world, allowing them to explore workshops, learn about traditional techniques, and experience the stories behind each crafted piece in a deeply personal way.

The launch of "Artisan Realms" was a momentous occasion, marked by an event that brought together artisans, investors, tech enthusiasts, and media. Jason and Kimberly, standing side by side, unveiled the platform, inviting guests to don VR headsets and step into the virtual marketplaces they had created.

The reaction was overwhelmingly positive. Users were captivated by the ability to virtually visit artisans' workshops across the globe, gaining an appreciation for the skill, tradition, and culture embedded in each piece. For the artisans, the platform offered a new way to showcase their work, reaching a wider audience than ever before and forging meaningful connections with consumers interested in the stories and sustainability behind their purchases.

However, the success of "Artisan Realms" was not just measured in user engagement or sales. For Jason and Kimberly, the true victory was in the feedback from the artisan community. Many artisans expressed how being part of this project had not only increased their visibility and income but had also instilled a sense of pride and validation in their work. The platform was more than a marketplace; it was a celebration of creativity and cultural heritage. .

In the wake of the launch, Jason and Kimberly reflected on the journey of "Artisan Realms." They recognized that this project was a significant step forward in their mission but also understood that it was just one milestone in a continuing journey. The challenges they faced in developing and launching the VR platform had tested their resolve, creativity, and partnership, strengthening their commitment to each other and their shared vision.

CHAPTER 23

GLOBAL THREADS, PERSONAL WEAVES

The success of "Artisan Realms" propelled Jason and Kimberly's startup into a new echelon of global social enterprises. The platform not only revolutionized how people engaged with artisanal crafts but also set a new standard for how technology could be used to preserve and promote cultural heritage. As the platform grew, so did their responsibility to the artisans and communities they served, prompting them to embark on a series of initiatives aimed at expanding their impact.

One such initiative was the establishment of the "Global Artisan Fund," a program designed to support artisans in developing their skills, expanding their workshops, and sustaining their cultural practices. This fund was a direct response to the needs articulated by the artisan community, ensuring that their success was shared and that the benefits of "Artisan Realms" extended beyond the digital realm.

As they worked to expand the platform, integrating new artisan communities from different parts of the world, Jason and Kimberly faced the challenge of maintaining the authenticity and integrity of the experience. Each new community brought its own set of traditions, stories, and struggles, requiring a nuanced approach to representation and support. This expansion was a delicate balancing act, one that tested their commitment to ethical and sustainable practices.

Amidst this period of rapid growth and change, the personal dynamics between Jason and Kimberly evolved. The couple found themselves in the public eye more than ever before, their relationship subjected to the scrutiny and pressures that came with success. They navigated these challenges with openness and honesty, relying on the strong foundation of trust and mutual respect they had built over the years.

Their personal journey took a new turn when they decided to document their travels and interactions with artisan communities in a series of short films. These films, intended as a behind-the-scenes look at the making of "Artisan Realms," offered a personal glimpse into Jason and Kimberly's journey, highlighting the deep connections they formed with artisans, the transformative power of their work and their unfiltered affection which was very visible on screen.

The launch of these films added a new dimension to their platform, humanizing the technology and bringing the stories of artisans to the forefront. It also allowed Jason and Kimberly to share their vision and values with a wider audience, inspiring others to consider how technology and business could be leveraged for social good.

After a wave of attention from their short films, Kimberly noticed a lack of security and the constant need to drive around, which put a lot of strain on both her and Jason.

"Jason, with all this new attention, I'm really worried about our security. Plus, all this driving around is exhausting," Kimberly said, rubbing her temples.

Jason nodded in agreement. "I feel the same way. We need a reliable driver and someone to ensure our safety." Jason offered a solution. "I know just the person. Mr. Patel, an old friend of my dad. He's incredibly skilled and trustworthy."

Kimberly's face brightened. "That sounds like exactly what we need."Jason smiled, hugged Kimberly, and kissed her. "I'll introduce you to him tomorrow."

The introduction was made, and Mr. Patel, along with his wife, quickly became a valuable part of their team. With his help, Jason and Kimberly could focus more on their work, knowing they were safe and had reliable transportation.

CHAPTER 24

WOVEN FUTURES

The global summit had been a resounding success, not just in terms of attendance and engagement, but in the depth of conversations it sparked. Discussions ranged from the preservation of traditional crafts in the digital age to the role of technology in fostering global communities. The summit concluded with the establishment of a collaborative network, aimed at supporting artisan communities worldwide through knowledge sharing, resources, and technology.

In the weeks following the summit, the short films released by Jason and Kimberly began to make waves beyond their immediate network. These films, with their intimate portrayal of artisan lives and the couple's journey, resonated with audiences globally, drawing attention to the significance of cultural preservation and the potential of ethical business practices. The films not only brought new users to "Artisan Realms" but also attracted the attention of documentary filmmakers and media outlets, further amplifying their message.

Amid this growing attention, Jason and Kimberly took a moment to reflect on their journey and plan for the future. They recognized the importance of maintaining the platform's authenticity and integrity as it scaled. This meant rigorous vetting of new artisan communities, continuous dialogue with existing ones, and a commitment to environmentally sustainable practices in all aspects of their operation.

Their personal relationship, always the bedrock of their partnership, had evolved in tandem with their business. The shared experiences, challenges, and successes had deepened their connection, reinforcing their commitment to each other and to their journey. They made a conscious decision to ensure that, no matter the demands of their growing venture, they would preserve time for themselves, for adventure, and for reflection.

Looking ahead, Jason and Kimberly began to outline the next phase of their strategic plan. This included leveraging the growing interest in their short films to launch an educational initiative aimed at schools and universities, raising awareness about cultural preservation and social entrepreneurship among younger generations. They also planned to explore new technologies that could further enhance the "Artisan Realms" experience, such as augmented reality (AR) for educational purposes and blockchain for transparency in artisan transactions.

CHAPTER 25

INNOVATING LEGACY

The launch of the educational initiative marked a significant milestone for Jason and Kimberly. They had always envisioned "Artisan Realms" as more than a marketplace—it was to be a platform for education and advocacy for cultural preservation. Partnering with educational institutions, they developed a curriculum that used their platform and documentaries as tools to teach students about global cultures, entrepreneurship, and sustainability.

This initiative quickly gained traction, with educators praising the engaging and immersive nature of the content. Students were not only learning about global artisan communities but were also inspired to think about how technology could be used to solve real-world problems. For Jason and Kimberly, the initiative was a realization of their belief that change begins with education and understanding.

Simultaneously, their exploration into augmented reality (AR) began to bear fruit. The AR feature allowed users to visualize artisan products in their own space, bridging the gap between the digital and physical realms. More than just a tool for enhancing user experience, the AR functionality served as an educational bridge, providing deeper insights into the cultural significance and craftsmanship of each piece.

The integration of blockchain technology introduced a new level of transparency and trust to the platform. Each artisan product was accompanied by a digital passport, detailing its origin, the story of its creator, and the journey it had taken. This innovation not only empowered consumers with knowledge but also celebrated the artisans' work, ensuring fair compensation and recognition for their skills.

As these new features were rolled out, Jason and Kimberly faced the challenge of maintaining the platform's user-friendly nature while integrating complex technologies. It was a delicate balancing act, requiring continuous feedback from users and artisans alike. Their commitment to community engagement ensured that "Artisan Realms" remained a platform that was accessible, informative, and empowering.

Personal growth paralleled their professional achievements. The success of their initiatives brought new challenges, but also new opportunities for learning and self-reflection. Jason and Kimberly found themselves increasingly in the role of mentors and advocates for social entrepreneurship, sharing their journey and insights at conferences and workshops around the world.

Despite the demands of their growing venture, they remained committed to their personal well-being and relationship. They understood that their strength as partners was the foundation of their success, and they nurtured this aspect of their lives with as much intention as they did their business.

CHAPTER 26

A NEW CHAPTER BEGINS

In the warmth of a serene morning, Jason and Kimberly sat on the veranda of their home, overlooking the lush landscape that had been the backdrop of their love story and entrepreneurial journey. With cups of coffee in hand, they shared a comfortable silence, each lost in thought about the future. The air was filled with a sense of anticipation, a prelude to the conversation they both knew was coming.

Kimberly broke the silence, her voice soft but resolute. "I've been thinking about us, about our journey, and about what's next. Not just for 'Artisan Realms,' but for us, personally." She paused, gauging Jason's reaction.

Jason set his cup down and smiled, turning to face her fully. "I've been thinking the same. We've built something incredible together, something that's changed not just our lives but the lives of so many others. But I feel like there's a piece of our story that's still waiting to be written."

The unspoken thought between them, the idea of starting a family, had been a gentle undercurrent in their lives. Now, as they faced each other, it surged to the forefront, tangible and urgent.

"We've talked about it before, but I think it's time," Kimberly continued, her hand finding Jason's. "I believe we're ready to start a family, to bring a new life into this world and into the midst of our journey."

Jason's response was a smile, warm and embracing, reflecting his agreement and excitement. "I think so, too. We have so much love to give, and I can't imagine a better adventure than raising a child with you. Our work is important, but this... this feels like the next chapter we're meant to embark on."

Their decision to start a family was not made lightly. They knew the challenges of balancing their demanding roles with parenting, but they also recognized the strength of their partnership. They had navigated the complexities of building a global venture from the ground up; they could navigate the complexities of parenthood.

As they discussed what this new chapter would mean, Jason and Kimberly were pragmatic. They spoke of timelines, of integrating their personal aspirations with their professional responsibilities, and of the support systems they would need to put in place. They envisioned a future where their child would grow up surrounded by a diverse, global community, learning from the rich variety of cultures and stories that "Artisan Realms" had brought into their lives.

The conversation shifted towards how they could ensure their venture continued to thrive and evolve, even as they took steps back to focus on their family. They talked about empowering their team, about strategic planning, and about setting in place structures that would allow the business to operate smoothly in their lessened day-to-day involvement.

As the day gave way to evening, Jason and Kimberly's conversation turned to dreams and hopes for their child. They imagined a child who would inherit their curiosity, their passion for making a difference, and their love for the world's diverse cultures. A child who would, in their own way, continue the legacy of innovation, compassion, and global community that they had built.

CHAPTER 27

WELCOME, O'BRIAN

The journey to parenthood was a tempest of emotions for Jason and Kimberly, marred by heartbreak and frustration before it reached its joyful crescendo with the birth of O'Brian. Their path had been fraught with trials; after two miscarriages in less than two years, the pain and disappointment had taken a heavy toll on Kimberly. Each loss was a storm they weathered together, but it left Kimberly teetering on the edge of despair.

One evening, in a moment heavy with emotion, Kimberly turned to Jason, her voice thick with frustration and a resolve that had been hard-earned through their struggles. "Jason, I... I can't keep doing this," she confessed, the weight of her words hanging in the air between them. "I'll try just one more time, but I can't... that's it. That's all I have left in me."

Jason, ever her pillar of strength, wrapped his arms around her, understanding the depth of her pain. "I'm with you, my love," he assured her, his voice steady yet laced with his own heartache. "No matter what happens, we're in this together."

And then, against the backdrop of their shared dreams and amidst the trials that had tested their resolve, O'Brian's arrival marked a turning point. His first cry in the early hours of the morning was a symphony of hope and pure joy that was heard loud and strong by his extended family and close family friends in the waiting room. In the delivery room it was a sound so sweet and so longed-for that it seemed to heal some of the fractures in his parents' hearts. O'Brian wasn't just a child; he was a beacon of a new chapter, both personally and professionally, for Jason and Kimberly.

As O'Brian grew, his curiosity and intelligence became a source of endless wonder for his parents. His keen observations and questions about the world around him sparked conversations filled with discovery and learning. Jason and Kimberly, despite the demands of their venture, were devoted parents, eager to share the stories and cultures behind the artisan crafts that filled their home. O'Brian's nursery, adorned with pieces from across the globe, was a testament to their life's work and the diversity of cultures they celebrated.

O'Brian's relentless "Why?" became the soundtrack of their lives, pushing Jason and Kimberly to explore and explain the world in ways they never had before. His innocence and eagerness to learn reminded them of the essence of their mission with "Artisan Realms"—to bridge cultures and generations through the stories embedded in artisan crafts.

Balancing entrepreneurship with parenting brought its challenges, but O'Brian added a richness to their lives that made every struggle worth it. He became the heart of their mission, embodying the connection and curiosity that "Artisan Realms" sought to inspire in the world.

The sleepless nights and the constant juggle of responsibilities were dwarfed by the joy and fulfillment

O'Brian brought into their lives. He was not just a part of their present but a beacon for the future, embodying the promise of growth and continuity for their family and their broader mission. Jason and Kimberly looked forward to the day O'Brian would not only inherit "Artisan Realms" but also infuse it with his own creativity and vision, continuing the legacy they had begun.

CHAPTER 28

BALANCING ACTS

In the vibrant world of "Artisan Realms," the birth of O'Brian heralded a new era for Jason and Kimberly, weaving a fresh pattern into the fabric of their lives. Their existence, once fully engrossed in the cultivation of their venture and its community, now pulsed with the vibrant energy of parenthood, a journey filled with both the chaos and bliss of balancing their professional dreams with the demands of family life.

The spirit of exploration and discovery that defined "Artisan Realms" flourished anew within the walls of their home, spurred by O'Brian's boundless curiosity. Each day unfurled with his questions, turning meals into impromptu seminars on everything from the intricacies of their digital platform to the rich histories of the artisan pieces that dotted their living spaces. These interactions were more than just opportunities to satisfy his curiosity; they were moments to sow the seeds of innovation, ethical integrity, and a profound appreciation for cultural diversity in O'Brian's growing mind.

Committed to embodying these principles in every facet of their lives, Jason and Kimberly adeptly navigated their dual roles at "Artisan Realms" and as parents. They took turns steering the helm of their business and dedicating uninterrupted time to O'Brian, ensuring he grew up feeling the full presence of their love and attention. They introduced him to their team and made "Artisan Realms" a second home for him, where he was embraced by a community that shared tales and laughter, fostering a sense of belonging and shared purpose from an early age.

O'Brian's presence at the office or during visits to artisan workshops symbolized the merging of digital innovation with traditional craftsmanship. These moments were precious lessons on the value of ethical business practices, as Jason and Kimberly demonstrated the power of technology in creating a positive societal impact, teaching O'Brian that true success was measured in the lives touched and improved through their work.

Kimberly, a master storyteller, captivated O'Brian with tales of the artisans behind their crafts. These stories, rich with empathy, diversity, and perseverance, were not merely bedtime stories but life lessons aimed at nurturing a deep respect for cultural richness and the endless potential of human creativity.

Jason, meanwhile, fostered a love for inquiry and innovation in O'Brian, encouraging him to explore, question, and create. They bonded over small projects, from assembling gadgets to dabbling in coding, embedding the joys of discovery and the importance of thinking outside the box in O'Brian's malleable mind.

Juggling the demands of "Artisan Realms" with the responsibilities of parenting was a formidable feat, filled with days when the weight of deadlines and the scale of their ambition seemed insurmountable. Yet, the journey from struggling to conceive to embracing the joys and trials of parenthood had fortified Jason and Kimberly with resilience, adaptability, and an unshakeable partnership. Supported by their team, and buoyed by a network of family and friends, they navigated the complexities of nurturing both a family and a global venture with grace, embodying the very essence of community, innovation, and shared humanity that "Artisan Realms" sought to promote.

CHAPTER 29

EARLY GENIUS

As O'Brian matured into his teenage years, the complexity of his intellect and the vastness of his curiosity unfolded like the beginning chapters of an epic novel brimming with potential. His upbringing, in a home where the whispers of technology intertwined seamlessly with the vibrant stories of global artistry, set the stage for an extraordinary adolescence. As a teen O'Brian's thirst for knowledge had only deepened, fueled by the rich legacy of innovation and cultural appreciation his parents had instilled in him.

One quiet evening, amidst the creative chaos of their living room, O'Brian, now 14, was engrossed in the intricate task of reassembling a vintage computer. His concentration was intense, his hands moving with precision over the components. Jason observed with a mixture of admiration and nostalgia.

"It's incredible, you know," Jason mused aloud, "You've got your mom's focus and passion. She could get lost for days in her creative projects, just like you with these machines."

Before Kimberly could add her thoughts, Marlene, O'Brian's grandmother, chimed in with a chuckle, her eyes twinkling with memories of the past. "Oh, Jason was very much like you at your age, O'Brian. Always tinkering, always curious. There wasn't a gadget in the house he didn't take apart just to see how it worked. You're carrying on a fine tradition, my boy."

O'Brian looked up, his interest piqued. It was one thing to know his parents' present interests and achievements, but hearing about his father's childhood adventures added a new layer of connection to his own experiences.

"In my own way, I was," Kimberly added, stepping into the room, her presence still marked by the day's artistic endeavors. "Art was my realm, but I always admired your dad's knack for bringing technology to life. It seems you've inherited the best of both worlds."

This blend of passions had nurtured O'Brian's distinctive talents. He was not content with mere play; he sought to unravel the mechanisms behind his gadgets, driven by the same curiosity that led him to absorb the stories and cultures behind the art that filled their home.

His relentless inquiries, a barrage of "Why?" and "How?" enriched the family's daily life, each question a testament to the ever-expanding horizon of his understanding.

School presented a unique set of challenges and triumphs for O'Brian. Academically, he was unmatched, often venturing far beyond the curriculum. His true achievement, however, lay in the synthesis of his interests. For a project on ancient civilizations, O'Brian crafted a digital exhibit that wove together technology and storytelling, creating an immersive experience that breathed life into history.

His project was a revelation to his teachers, a curiosity to his classmates, and a source of wonder for Jason and Kimberly. "You're charting new territories, O'Brian," Kimberly observed, her voice tinged with pride. "You've found a way to make art and technology converse in a language that's uniquely yours."

Yet, O'Brian's exceptional intellect sometimes placed him on the periphery of his peer group, a solitude that was both a sanctuary and a chasm. Despite this, he found comfort in his pursuits, in the boundless realms of ideas where he could wander freely, unencumbered by the confines of conventional adolescent interactions.

CHAPTER 30

LEGACY OF KNOWLEDGE

The sun had barely risen, casting a soft glow over the bustling household of Jason and Kimberly. Amid the quiet hum of the early morning, a distinct air of anticipation filled their home. Today marked a significant milestone in O'Brian's life—the day he would formally step into the world his parents had built: "Artisan Realms."

O'Brian, now more aware of the world around him and brimming with questions, had shown an increasing interest in his parents' work. Recognizing his budding curiosity, Jason and Kimberly decided it was time to introduce him to the intricacies of their platform and the global community they served.

After breakfast, the family gathered in their home office, a room lined with artifacts and state-of-the-art technology—a fusion of the past and the future. Jason started the session by pulling up the "Artisan Realms" platform on the screen, the colorful   websites coming to life before O'Brian's eager eyes.

Kimberly began, "O'Brian, this is 'Artisan Realms,' a place where artisans from around the world share their crafts and stories. Your dad and I started this with a dream—to connect people through art and culture."

Jason took over, navigating through the platform, showcasing different artisan profiles. "Each of these artisans have a unique story, a family, a community they support through their work. 'Artisan Realms' helps them reach people they never could have before."

O'Brian, fascinated, watched as his parents demonstrated how the platform worked. They explained the technology behind it, the importance of a user-friendly interface, and how blockchain ensures transparency and trust in transactions.

Kimberly shared stories of specific artisans, highlighting the impact "Artisan Realms" had on their lives. She spoke of a weaver in Guatemala who was now able to afford her daughter's education, a potter in Morocco who had revitalized a dying craft in his village, and a jewelry maker in Kenya who employed dozens of local women, providing them with a steady income.

The discussion shifted to the challenges—ethical sourcing, ensuring fair compensation, and the constant battle against cultural appropriation. Jason emphasized, "Our work is about respect, O'Brian. We're not just selling products; we're sharing cultures. It's a delicate balance, maintaining integrity while growing a global business."

As the day progressed, O'Brian's role became more hands-on. Jason and Kimberly involved him in a simple task—curating a collection of artisan stories for the next newsletter. Guided by his parents, O'Brian selected stories that resonated with him, learning the importance of storytelling in connecting people.

CHAPTER 31

THE FIRST SIGNS OF LEADERSHIP

As O'Brian navigated his teenage years, a distinct blend of leadership qualities and problem-solving abilities began to emerge, distinguishing him in the structured yet expansive realm of adolescence. This particular summer, a unique initiative by "Artisan Realms" provided the perfect backdrop for these traits to shine, highlighting O'Brian's growing influence and hinting at the significant role he was destined to play in the venture's future.

"Artisan Realms" had launched a summer project aimed at engaging teenagers in understanding and supporting global artisan communities. Eager to contribute, 15-year-old O'Brian quickly transitioned from participant to leader among his peers. His knack for listening, gathering diverse ideas, and steering towards innovative solutions was remarkable, catching the attention of Jason, Kimberly, and the wider "Artisan Realms" team.

Jason and Kimberly were filled with pride and a touch of awe as they observed O'Brian's effortless navigation of his newfound role. In brainstorming sessions, he had a special way of ensuring everyone felt heard, all while guiding the group to meaningful and productive outcomes. His insights were not just reflective of his intelligence but also of his deep connection to the "Artisan Realms" mission, a demonstration of his upbringing in a world where creativity and global awareness were daily bread.

The summer project faced a challenge in making the idea of cultural preservation engaging and understandable to a young, diverse audience. Despite various suggestions, the team struggled to find a concept that resonated. It was then that O'Brian, with his fresh perspective, proposed a novel idea: creating a collaborative art and tech workshop. Instead of a virtual world tour, this workshop would invite teenagers to use technology to create art that tells the stories of artisans around the world.

This suggestion was both surprising and inspiring. It was perfectly aligned with the project's educational goals, it was innovative, and it addressed the challenge head-on. O'Brian's proposal not only offered a solution but also enriched the campaign with an interactive, hands-on component that promised to deepen participants' engagement.

O'Brian's journey through the summer initiative was not without its challenges. A few of his team members were jealous of him taking the spotlight. When nobody was looking, they walked up to him and confronted him.

"Why are you always taking the spotlight?" one of them sneered. "You only feel smart because your parents are the creators of the initiative. Your ideas are foolish, and if it wasn't for your parents, they wouldn't have been acknowledged."

Though this type of interaction was not uncommon, it still left him feeling down and angry, O'Brian walked away from the group. Mr. Patel, a mentor in the program and a family friend, noticed the exchange and approached O'Brian, offering a small pep talk.

"You are very smart, just like your parents," he said. "You should ignore them. They are just a little jealous, and that's what kids do sometimes."

Mr. Patel's words resonated with O'Brian, motivating him even more to prove his worth and show that he could stand on his own merits.

As the project progressed, O'Brian's involvement became increasingly central. With support from his parents and the "Artisan Realms" team, he helped develop his workshop idea into a tangible program. His active participation in shaping the workshop, providing feedback, and even facilitating sessions, showcased his commitment and leadership.

The campaign's success, buoyed by O'Brian's innovative approach, was a cause for celebration within the "Artisan Realms" community. It was evident that O'Brian had not only inherited his parents' intellect and passion but also their flair for leadership and creativity. His ability to devise solutions that were both engaging and impactful left a lasting impression, marking him as a burgeoning leader with a bright future ahead.

CHAPTER 32

A FAMILY VENTURE

The world of "Artisan Realms" had always been more than just a business for Jason and Kimberly—it was a vision, a mission, and now, more than ever, a family venture. With O'Brian showing an ever-deepening interest in their work and his emerging skills in leadership and problem-solving, Jason and Kimberly saw an invaluable opportunity to blend their professional journeys with personal growth and family bonding. They decided to embark on a series of travels for "Artisan Realms" projects, making each trip an enriching educational experience for O'Brian.

The first stop on their trip took them to a remote village in Peru, home to a community of weavers whose intricate textiles told stories of generations. For O'Brian, the trip was an adventure, an opportunity to see, first-hand, the cultures and crafts he had only read about or seen through the digital window of "Artisan Realms." For Jason and Kimberly, it was a chance to deepen their son's understanding of the mission at the heart of their work and to witness the real-world impact of what they did.

Each day in Peru was a new lesson for O'Brian. He learned about the traditional techniques passed down through generations, the natural dyes that painted the vibrant textiles, and the stories interwoven into every pattern. He watched his parents engage with the artisans, not just as business partners but as learners and admirers of their craft. These interactions, rich with respect and mutual learning, underscored for O'Brian the values of cultural appreciation and ethical collaboration that his parents upheld.

The family's travels did not stop in Peru. They visited craftsmen in Morocco, potters in Japan, and beadwork artists in South Africa, each destination adding layers to O'Brian's understanding of the world's cultural diversity and the universal language of art. With each journey, O'Brian's role evolved from observer to participant. He began to engage with the artisans, asking questions, and even trying his hand at various crafts, guided by the skilled hands of master artisans.

These experiences were transformative for O'Brian. He began to see "Artisan Realms" not just as his parents' business but as a global family of creators and innovators. He understood the platform's power to connect disparate worlds, to bring visibility to underrepresented cultures, and to create sustainable opportunities for artisans. This understanding deepened his sense of responsibility toward the venture and its global community.

For Jason and Kimberly, watching O'Brian grow through these experiences was a reaffirmation of their decision to integrate him into the fabric of "Artisan Realms." They saw him developing not just knowledge and skills but a profound sense of empathy and a genuine desire to make a difference.

CHAPTER 33

THE WORLD THROUGH HIS EYES

In the ever-evolving narrative of "Artisan Realms," a digital haven born from the vision and perseverance of Jason and Kimberly, a novel concept was about to unfold, courtesy of their son, O'Brian. Now a reflective adolescent, O'Brian was poised to infuse new vitality into the legacy meticulously crafted by his parents.

On a serene Saturday afternoon, amidst the family's collection of global artifacts that whispered tales of diverse cultures, the "Artisan Realms" team—Jason, Kimberly, and O'Brian—convened in their bright living room. Such family gatherings had always been a cradle for the platform's most sincere innovations. This time, it was O'Brian who had sparked the assembly, eager to share the insights that had been simmering in his mind.

"While diving into my digital platforms project," O'Brian started, his enthusiasm barely contained, "it hit me. 'Artisan Realms' isn't just a marketplace. It's a gateway to immersive cultural experiences. We have a chance to deepen our engagement, to not just showcase artisan crafts but to truly envelop our users in the artisans' worlds."

Jason and Kimberly listened, intrigued, sensing the emergence of a groundbreaking idea from their son. "Tell us more," Jason prompted, a proponent of innovation and forward-thinking.

Buoyed by his father's encouragement, O'Brian expanded on his vision. "We already have an AR system, right? But what if we took it further? Users could explore an artisan's studio in real-time, watch them create, understand the cultural context of each piece, and listen to the artisan's personal narrative through augmented reality."

The room quieted as they grasped the magnitude of O'Brian's proposal—a visionary blend of technology and tradition that could redefine "Artisan Realms."

Kimberly, with her artistic sensibility, was quick to see the beauty in the idea. "That's not just innovative, O'Brian; it's transformative. Each craft becomes a gateway, offering a glimpse into another life, another culture."

Jason, contemplating the technical aspects, saw both challenge and opportunity. "Integrating this advanced AR could be complex, but it's feasible. We might need to collaborate with specialists in AR technology and involve our artisans more deeply to capture the essence of their stories."

The discussion that ensued was electric, a cascade of ideas enriching O'Brian's initial spark. Each family member added their unique perspective, weaving a richer blend of possibilities.

As the conversation wound down, O'Brian was awash with a sense of accomplishment and excitement. His concept, once a mere flicker of inspiration, was now on the brink of becoming a revolutionary feature of "Artisan Realms," illustrating the invaluable impact of new perspectives and the power of collaboration.

CHAPTER 34

BONDS OF LOVE

The aroma of coffee wafted through the air on a tranquil Saturday morning, mingling with bursts of laughter and relaxed chatter that echoed through the family home. Jason was at the helm in the kitchen, expertly flipping pancakes—a cherished part of their weekend routine—while Kimberly prepared the dining table, laying out utensils in anticipation of the hearty breakfast that would fuel their day ahead.

O'Brian, now 16 and brimming with curiosity, poured the different beverages - coffee for his dad, tea for his mother and juice for himself then took his place at the table. As he awaited the steamy delicious pancakes he scrolled through his phone while half listening to his mother chattering away about the day's plans. The family had a simple yet promising agenda: a visit to a local art exhibit, a trek through the beauty of nature, and an evening dedicated to storytelling, where they would share tales from their travels and the diverse cultures that had touched their lives.

Their hike was an adventure, with O'Brian leading the charge. His energy and inquisitive nature turned every moment into a discovery. He was especially fascinated by the various fungi they encountered along the way. He even took different mushroom samples to bring to his lab attached to his room.

As he moved about, lost in his own world of unearthing and discovering, his parents watched on with joy and pride. Often inquiring about his findings.

"What have you found this time, son?" Jason asked.

"I think I found a species of mushroom that isn't indigenous to our ecosystem," replied O'Brian, still captivated by his new discovery.

Jason smiled. "That's amazing, buddy."

Kimberly came closer. "Wow, this is so beautiful, O'Brian."

O'Brian's quiet excitement was infectious, and his parents couldn't help but be drawn into his world of wonder. These simple pleasures reminded Jason and Kimberly of the joy of being present.

By the time they returned from the hike, the family was enveloped in a mix of tiredness and satisfaction, their bodies weary but spirits high from the day's explorations. Hunger pangs made themselves known, heightening the anticipation for the feast that awaited them.

The Patels, bringing a taste of Cuba to the gathering, had prepared a batch of empanadas, filled with spiced meats and vegetables, and a side of tostones, crispy and lightly salted. Marlene contributed her famous mac and cheese, a dish so creamy and comforting it had become a legend in the family. Together, the leftover pancakes, empanadas, tostones, and mac and cheese created a multicultural spread that was a testament to the diversity and warmth of their community.

The art exhibit offered another layer to their day of discovery. O'Brian's observations and questions sparked discussions on creativity, expression, and the stories behind the art, enriching the family's experience and deepening their connection.

As night fell, they gathered in the coziness of their living room, the soft candlelight setting the perfect atmosphere for their tradition of storytelling. This intimate gathering was a time to share not just stories of their travels but also reflections on their dreams, fears, and the lessons they had learned. O'Brian, inspired by the tales of far-off lands, felt his imagination soar, enveloped in the shared laughter and love that filled the room.

Enhancing the evening were Jason's mother, Marlene, his sister, Leah, and their close family friends, Mr. and Mrs. Patel from Cuba. Marlene reminisced about Jason's childhood adventures, Leah talked about her latest art projects, and the Patels shared stories from their Cuban heritage. Each narrative added to the evening's richness, creating an atmosphere of wisdom, humor, and cultural depth. This gathering, vibrant with stories and affection, was a living testament to the essence of "Artisan Realms"—a community bound by creativity, curiosity, and an enduring bond of love, celebrating stories that span continents and cultures.

CHAPTER 35

TRAGEDY STRIKES

On a serene Monday morning, the family home was enveloped in a quiet anticipation, the kind that precedes a significant journey. Jason and Kimberly were abuzz with preparations, their spirits lifted by the prospect of attending an international summit in France. This wasn't just any summit; it was a convergence of minds passionate about blending technology and art for social good, an ethos at the heart of "Artisan Realms."

As they packed, their conversation fluttered around the opportunities this summit promised—new partnerships, inspiration, and perhaps, a chance to showcase "Artisan Realms" on a global stage. Yet, this trip was special for another reason; Jason's parents and his sister Leah were coming along. Having never visited France, this was a perfect opportunity to mix work and vacation, an experience Jason and Kimberly were thrilled to share with them.

O'Brian, engrossed in his project that mirrored his parents' innovative spirit, looked up as Kimberly reminded him of their imminent departure. "Remember, Mr. and Mrs. Patel will be here for you. And we'll call once we land," she assured, her voice carrying a mix of excitement and maternal concern.

"I'll be fine, Mom," O'Brian responded, his smile a brave front. "Focus on the summit. It's a big opportunity for 'Artisan Realms.' I've got this."

Jason tousled O'Brian's hair with affection, pride in his resilience. "Just don't forget to have some fun too, okay?"

Their departure was marked by heartfelt goodbyes, a moment of familial warmth amidst the rush of travel. Yet, the world shifted irrevocably the next day. A call in the early hours brought devastating news—the plane carrying Jason, Kimberly, and his family had crashed, leaving no survivors.

The loss was a blow that reverberated through the core of O'Brian's world, plunging the family home into a somber state as friends, family, and the "Artisan Realms" community came together in grief. Among them, Mr. and Mrs. Patel, the pillars of support Jason and Kimberly had always trusted, stepped in to anchor O'Brian in the turbulent wake of tragedy.

In the days that followed, as condolences poured in and stories of Jason and Kimberly's vibrant lives and legacy were shared, the weight of loss and the daunting path forward loomed large for O'Brian. The Patels, embodying the familial bond and community spirit that "Artisan Realms" was built upon, offered solace and guidance.

One quiet evening, amidst the remnants of his parents' dreams and endeavors, O'Brian found solace in a conversation with Mr. Patel. "Your parents were extraordinary, O'Brian. They've left an indelible mark on the world and on you. They believed in you, in your strength to carry forward their vision," Mr. Patel said, his voice a comforting balm.

Confronted with the enormity of his loss and the legacy left in his hands, O'Brian confided, "I'm not sure I can live up to their legacy."

Mr. Patel's response was firm and reassuring, "You're not alone, O'Brian. This community, your family, we're here to support you. Your parents' legacy is strong, and so are you. They've prepared you for this, even if it doesn't feel like it right now. Together, we'll continue what they started. You have their spirit, their determination. And that will guide you through."

In the quiet aftermath of those words, O'Brian felt the first stirrings of resolve. With the support of the "Artisan Realms" community and the foundational values his parents instilled in him, he began to envision a path forward, one step at a time, toward upholding and evolving the legacy of innovation, creativity, and community his parents had cherished.

CHAPTER 36

LEGACY AND LOSS

In the wake of the accident, O'Brian's world felt like it was suspended in a state of disbelief. Mornings would come, and for a fleeting moment, he'd anticipate the familiar sounds of his parents in the kitchen, their laughter permeating the air, only to be met with silence—a harsh reminder of the void their absence had left.

The once lively home, a testament to creativity and love, now echoed with quietness that seemed too vast, too profound. Yet, in this sea of silence, Mr. and Mrs. Patel became O'Brian's anchor. One evening, amidst the remnants of memories and dreams woven into the fabric of their home, Mr. Patel broached a conversation that loomed heavy on their hearts.

"O'Brian," he began, kindness threading through his words, "the loss you're facing... It's immeasurable. Your parents were extraordinary, leaving behind a legacy that touched countless lives, including ours. It's a legacy that lives on, through 'Artisan Realms,' through you."

O'Brian, his gaze lingering on a family photo, acknowledged the weight of Mr. Patel's words. "I keep thinking about what they would have wanted for me, for 'Artisan Realms.' I feel this immense pressure to uphold what they've built, to ensure their dreams don't fade away. But I'm scared... scared I might not be up to the task."

Mrs. Patel, with a gesture of warmth, took his hand, offering solace. "They believed in you, O'Brian, more than anything. They saw the potential in you to carry on their aspirations, their values. And remember, you're not alone. We're here for you, as is the entire 'Artisan Realms' community. It's natural to feel daunted, to need time to find your footing."

Their conversation was gently interrupted by a call from the "Artisan Realms" team. With encouragement from Mrs. Patel, O'Brian answered, greeted by the faces of those who had worked closely with his parents, each expressing their support and readiness to stand by him.

"We've been thinking, O'Brian," a team leader shared through the screen, "and we're here to reaffirm our commitment to the vision your parents set forth. 'Artisan Realms' is more than a business; it's a community, a movement. And we believe in its mission, in you. When you're ready, we'll be here to support and guide you."

This conversation, though tinged with sorrow, sparked a glimmer of hope within O'Brian. In the following days, he immersed himself in his parents' work, delving into their notes and future plans for "Artisan Realms." Each document, each written word, served as a testament to their dreams, igniting in O'Brian a clearer understanding of the path they had envisioned—not just for their venture but for him as well. Through this exploration, he began to connect more deeply with their vision, gradually embracing the role he was meant to play in continuing their legacy.

CHAPTER 37

STEPPING UP

Choosing to lead "Artisan Realms" was a decision that didn't come lightly for O'Brian. Night after night, he found himself wrestling with the enormity of stepping into his parents' shoes. Surrounded by the remnants of their legacy—old photographs, handwritten notes, and the early sketches of "Artisan Realms"—O'Brian felt the full weight of his responsibility. It was in these moments of solitude and reflection that he resolved to continue the mission his parents had so passionately pursued.

With the dawn breaking, O'Brian shared his decision with Mr. and Mrs. Patel, who had become much more than guardians in these trying times; they were his mentors, his pillars of strength. The kitchen, bathed in the morning's gentle light, felt like a safe haven as he voiced his intentions.

"I've spent a few months thinking about this," O'Brian confessed, his resolve shining through the uncertainty. "It's daunting, and I'm acutely aware of how much I need to learn. But I'm committed to continuing my parents' work with 'Artisan Realms.' It's not just about fulfilling their legacy—it's about believing in the vision we've nurtured as a family."

Mr. Patel, ever the voice of reason, acknowledged the challenge with a nod. "This journey you're choosing to embark on is significant, O'Brian. But remember, the foundation your parents laid is robust, and their vision has already touched many lives. You have a keen mind and a compassionate heart. And remember, you're not walking this path alone."

Mrs. Patel's warmth was palpable as she offered her support, "Your parents would have been overjoyed to see you take this step. We're here for you, and so is the 'Artisan Realms' team. They're an extension of your family, ready to stand by you."

Feeling heartened by their encouragement, O'Brian convened a meeting with the "Artisan Realms" team. Standing before a group that was a blend of old friends and new faces, he felt a surge of nervous energy. Yet, as he began to speak, a sense of purpose steadied him.

"I come before you, not as someone who has all the answers, but as someone who shares a deep belief in the mission of 'Artisan Realms,'" O'Brian shared openly. "I'm stepping into roles that my parents filled with love and dedication. I'm here to ask for your patience, your wisdom, and your support as we navigate the future together."

The team's response was a wave of solidarity. Encouraging words and commitments to the venture's future filled the space, reinforcing the sense of community that "Artisan Realms" represented. They recounted memories of Jason and Kimberly, reflecting on the journey from the venture's inception to its current standing, and reiterating their dedication to the vision that had guided its progress.

As days turned into weeks, O'Brian dedicated himself to learning the intricacies of "Artisan Realms," engaging with every facet of the business. He joined meetings, contributed to creative discussions, and sought insights from the artisans at the core of the platform. With each passing day, he felt his confidence grow, supported by the team and guided by the values his parents had championed. This journey, though fraught with challenges, was also one of discovery, affirming his commitment to leading "Artisan Realms" into its next chapter.

CHAPTER 38

A YOUNG CEO

O'Brian's inaugural day as the CEO of "Artisan Realms" marked the beginning of a significant new era, both for him personally and for the company his parents had lovingly developed. Stepping into the office, he carried the dual weight of responsibility and optimism, feeling the legacy of his role yet bolstered by the prospect of shaping the future.

Greeted by the team, their faces a reflection of the diverse and close-knit community his parents had established, O'Brian felt a renewed sense of purpose. The office, with its comforting blend of coffee aroma and the sheen of polished wood, felt like a launching pad for this new chapter.

The day unfolded with a flurry of activities—meetings that ran the gamut from operational briefings to strategic discussions, each moment a lesson in leadership and vision. O'Brian, in these early interactions, chose to listen, absorbing the collective wisdom around him, and learning to navigate the waters of his new role with grace.

A crucial meeting with the senior management team served as a litmus test for his leadership. Surrounded by seasoned professionals, each with their own ideas for the future of "Artisan Realms," O'Brian confronted his own insecurities. Was he ready to guide these individuals? Could he make decisions that would both honor his parents' memory and propel the company forward?

It was Mrs. Patel's voice that cut through his doubts, her encouragement, a well of wisdom.. "You're stepping into vast shoes, O'Brian, but remember, you're not expected to fill them on your own. We're here, alongside you, ready to support you in carving out your own path."

Emboldened by her words, O'Brian embraced a pivotal realization: true leadership was not about having all the answers but about fostering a shared vision and engaging the team in collective goal-setting.

One of his initial acts as CEO was to propose a project deeply resonant with his values—a digital archive for "Artisan Realms." This initiative aimed to chronicle the artisans' stories and crafts, a homage to his parents' dedication to storytelling and his personal passion for technology.

Presenting this concept to the team, O'Brian articulated his vision with clarity and conviction. "This archive is more than a preservation effort; it's a bridge to the future, using technology to maintain the vitality of these traditions. It's our tribute to the artisans, ensuring their legacy continues to enlighten and unite us."

The proposal was met with enthusiastic approval, sparking a collaborative endeavor that exemplified the collective ingenuity of the "Artisan Realms" team. This project became a focal point of O'Brian's early tenure, symbolizing a commitment to blending tradition with innovation.

As time passed, O'Brian tackled the challenges of leadership with humility and determination, facing each obstacle with the support of his team. Despite moments of doubt and debate, there were also breakthroughs and bonding, each step forward reinforcing his resolve to lead "Artisan Realms" into a promising future.

CHAPTER 39

BALANCING SCHOOL AND CEO DUTIES

Navigating the dual roles of high school student and CEO of "Artisan Realms" placed O'Brian in a uniquely challenging position. His days were a delicate balancing act—managing school responsibilities, steering a company forward, honoring his parents' legacy, and experiencing the trials and triumphs of adolescence.

One night, the strain of his double duties was particularly palpable. Surrounded by schoolbooks and corporate documents, O'Brian found himself caught between solving an algebra problem and addressing an important email from his team. The blue light from his laptop cast stark shadows across his concentrated face, highlighting the burden of his responsibilities.

Mrs. Patel, observing him quietly, voiced her concern with a wisdom and care that had become a comforting constant. "O'Brian, you're stretching yourself too thin. Your parents wanted you to thrive, not to be overwhelmed by responsibilities."

O'Brian sighed, leaning back in his chair. "I know Mrs. Patel, but I can't help feeling like I'm constantly falling short. At school, I'm the distracted student; at 'Artisan Realms,' I'm the inexperienced CEO. It's like I'm split in half, and neither side is getting the best of me."

It was at this moment that Mr. Patel, who had been walking by, paused to listen. Stepping into the room, he offered his perspective, having overheard the conversation. "O'Brian, the journey you're on is demanding, but it's also a testament to your strength. Maybe it's time to consider how we can better manage these responsibilities together."

Encouraged by Mr. Patel's intervention, they convened a family meeting to strategize and prioritize O'Brian's commitments. This gathering became a pivotal moment, providing O'Brian with a mix of practical advice, empathy, and understanding.

They devised a structured schedule that balanced schoolwork, CEO duties, and personal time, alongside instituting a weekly review session with the Patels. This approach allowed O'Brian to discuss his progress, confront challenges, and recalibrate his schedule as needed.

Furthermore, the Patels encouraged O'Brian to communicate openly with both his teachers and the "Artisan Realms" team about his unique situation. This led to an unexpected wave of support—teachers became more flexible with deadlines, and the team at "Artisan Realms" willingly took on additional responsibilities, lightening O'Brian's load.

Amid these changes, O'Brian found solace and a sense of belonging in his school's robotics club. There, he was just another student passionate about technology, a reprieve from the weight of expectations elsewhere. This club not only fostered his interest in technology but also allowed him to make friends, apply and refine his leadership skills, bridging his experiences between school and "Artisan Realms" in a way that enriched both aspects of his life.

CHAPTER 40

INNOVATIONS INSPIRED

O'Brian's tenure as the young CEO of "Artisan Realms" was marked by a fervent commitment to innovation, and honoring the legacy his parents, Jason and Kimberly, left behind. Among the flurry of responsibilities and the balance between his academic life and executive duties, he found a profound motivation to push the boundaries of what "Artisan Realms" could offer, inspired by his parents' forward-thinking ideas.

On a particularly reflective afternoon, O'Brian immersed himself in his parents' old journals and planners, which were brimming with ideas, sketches, and dreams yet to be realized. It was within these pages of visionary concepts that O'Brian discovered notes on enhancing the platform's existing virtual reality (VR) features with extended reality (XR) technology. This insight sparked a eureka moment for him.

Excited by the breakthrough, O'Brian convened a meeting with the "Artisan Realms" team. Standing in front of them, he felt a surge of energy, fueled by the anticipation of sharing something potentially transformative.

"Picture this," O'Brian proposed, his enthusiasm infectious, "a feature that transcends the current VR capabilities, bringing our users not just to the threshold of artisan workshops but inside them, through extended reality. XR can blend the digital and physical worlds, offering a more immersive, interactive experience. We can showcase the artisanal process, the cultural context, and the personal stories of the artisans in unparalleled depth."

The team was captivated by the idea, their engagement evident in the lively exchange that followed. They discussed the technical feasibility, the impact on user engagement, and how such a feature aligned with the company's mission of fostering deeper connections between artisans and the global community.

"It's exactly the kind of innovation your parents envisioned," remarked a team member, echoing a sentiment of admiration and support for O'Brian's vision. "Using cutting-edge technology to deepen cultural understanding and appreciation."

In the subsequent weeks, O'Brian and the team dedicated themselves to developing the XR feature. They delved into the intricacies of XR technology, focusing on creating a seamless, engaging user experience that honored the authenticity of each artisan's craft and story. O'Brian's hands-on leadership and commitment to his parents' values guided the project, blending technological innovation with a deep respect for cultural heritage.

The introduction of the XR studio to "Artisan Realms" was greeted with enthusiasm from both users and artisans. For users, the XR experiences offered a new dimension of engagement, providing an intimate glimpse into the artisans' processes and the stories behind their work. Artisans appreciated the innovative platform to share their heritage and craftsmanship more vividly with a global audience. O'Brian's vision for "Artisan Realms," fueled by the legacy of his parents and his drive for innovation, had taken a significant step forward, redefining the connection between technology, art, and culture.

CHAPTER 41

GLOBAL RECOGNITION

The launch of the XR studio within "Artisan Realms" marked a pivotal moment, transforming it from a mere marketplace to a groundbreaking platform that bridged the gap between artisans and a global audience. This initiative, spearheaded by O'Brian in honor of his parents, propelled "Artisan Realms" into the international limelight, embodying the fusion of technology and cultural preservation they had always envisioned.

As word of this innovative XR studio spread, the worlds of technology and cultural heritage took note. Invitations for O'Brian to share his insights and the story behind "Artisan Realms" began to arrive, from keynote speeches at renowned tech conferences to panels discussing the intersection of innovation and tradition. Each opportunity was a chance to highlight the unique mission and impact of "Artisan Realms."

On the eve of a significant tech conference, O'Brian found himself in his office, surrounded by the legacy of his parents' ambitions and the undoubted success of "Artisan Realms." Gazing at a photo of his parents, he felt a profound connection to their dreams. "We're making a difference," he murmured, a sense of accomplishment mingling with his longing for their presence. "I just wish you were here to see it," he continued.

The conference was a whirlwind of activity, drawing in a diverse crowd eager to learn about "Artisan Realms" and its pioneering XR studio. When O'Brian took the stage, the room was filled with anticipation. His introduction not only set the stage for a discussion on technology's role in cultural preservation but also paid homage to his parents' vision.

O'Brian's presentation detailed the journey of "Artisan Realms," emphasizing the transformative potential of the XR studio. He shared stories of artisans whose crafts and cultures were being celebrated and preserved in unprecedented ways, thanks to this new technology. The audience was captivated by the passion and vision behind "Artisan Realms," sparking an engaging Q&A session that delved into the intricacies of the XR platform and the broader implications for cultural heritage.

The conference culminated in O'Brian receiving an accolade for his innovative contributions to technology and social impact—a moment that underscored the significance of his work and the enduring influence of his parents' legacy.

In the aftermath of the conference, "Artisan Realms" witnessed a surge in interest and support. Collaborations with cultural institutions and tech companies blossomed, and the platform's mission was highlighted in media outlets worldwide. This newfound attention not only validated O'Brian's efforts but also underscored the global relevance of "Artisan Realms" and its commitment to connecting people with the richness of global cultures through technology. Coincidentally that day also marked his 23rd birthday. He spent it alone wishing he could have one of those birthdays from when his parents were around.

CHAPTER 42

NEW CHALLENGES

In the wake of "Artisan Realms'" ascent to global prominence under O'Brian's leadership, the platform faced a slew of unprecedented challenges. These ranged from operational strains due to rapid expansion, to intensified competition, and heightened scrutiny from both critics and admirers alike. O'Brian's innovative approach had catalyzed significant growth and opportunity but had also ushered in a period of complexity and challenge for the young CEO and his team.

During a crucial meeting convened to tackle these multifaceted issues, the atmosphere was thick with anticipation and the weight of responsibility. O'Brian, acutely aware of the stakes, outlined the myriad of challenges confronting "Artisan Realms," emphasizing the need for innovative solutions and strategic foresight to navigate the turbulent waters ahead.

The meeting took a dramatic turn when a senior manager, burdened by the pressure of the growing demands, voiced a sentiment that echoed the room's underlying tensions. "If your parents were here, this would've never happened," the manager remarked, a statement that momentarily cast a pall over the proceedings. The comment, while reflective of the stress the team was under, momentarily questioned O'Brian's capacity to steer the company in its ambitious direction.

Though momentarily stunned, O'Brian chose not to retaliate in kind but instead refocused the discussion on constructive solutions, showcasing his resolve to lead through adversity. However, the impact of the comment lingered, underscoring the challenges of leadership and the high expectations placed on O'Brian's shoulders.

Mrs. Patel, getting wind of the exchange, later advised O'Brian on the necessity of addressing the discord. Recognizing the truth in her counsel, O'Brian understood that direct confrontation and open dialogue were essential in maintaining leadership and authority, fostering a culture of mutual respect and transparency within "Artisan Realms."

In a subsequent one-on-one meeting with the senior manager, O'Brian navigated the delicate situation with a maturity that belied his years. He acknowledged the immense pressure the team was under but underscored the importance of unity and constructive communication in overcoming their challenges. "The comment made during our meeting, while born out of stress, was not conducive to our collective goals. My parents' legacy is the foundation upon which we build, but the responsibility to lead 'Artisan Realms' forward is mine," O'Brian expressed, his tone firm yet empathetic.

He continued, extending an olive branch and a practical solution to the underlying issues of resource strain that had contributed to the manager's frustration. "I understand the obstacles we face and the toll they take. To alleviate some of this pressure, I'll allocate additional resources to expand your team, ensuring we have the bandwidth to pursue our goals effectively and sustainably."

This measured approach not only resolved the immediate conflict but also reinforced the ethos of "Artisan Realms"—one that valued collaboration, empathy, and the pursuit of excellence. O'Brian's actions in the wake of the meeting demonstrated his commitment to upholding his parents' vision, his growth and maturity while also carving out his own path as the leader capable of guiding "Artisan Realms" through its most challenging yet potentially rewarding phase.

Through these trials, O'Brian's leadership was tested but ultimately strengthened. He emerged more determined to steer "Artisan Realms" with a blend of innovation, integrity, and inclusivity, embodying the values instilled by his parents and embraced by the entire "Artisan Realms" community.

CHAPTER 43

THE WEIGHT OF LEGACY

In the early morning hours, as daybreak gently nudged the world awake, O'Brian sought refuge in the legacy-filled office of his late parents, the founders of "Artisan Realms." Surrounded by mementos of their shared journey, he felt their guiding presence, urging him forward on a path they had once navigated together. This sacred space, a testament to their life's work, offered O'Brian both comfort and inspiration as he faced the dual challenges of preserving their legacy and steering "Artisan Realms" into the future.

Amidst this introspection, O'Brian whispered to the memories of Jason and Kimberly, expressing his longing for their wisdom. "I'm charting our course, guided by what you've taught me. Yet, the responsibility of honoring your vision while forging my own path is daunting," he admitted to the quiet room, seeking solace in their imagined counsel.

As dawn painted the room with light, O'Brian delved into his parents' journals, discovering not just their dreams but also their doubts. It was a profound reminder that uncertainty had also been their companion, yet never deterred their mission to connect cultures through "Artisan Realms." A remembered conversation with his mother resonated deeply, illuminating the essence of legacy—not merely the achievements left behind but the values imparted and the opportunities created for future generations.

Emboldened by this realization, O'Brian focused on an ambitious initiative that had long occupied his thoughts—a global artisan mentorship program. This program aimed to empower artisans by enhancing their craftsmanship and digital marketability, thus ensuring their traditions' sustainability and relevance. It was a harmonious extension of his parents' dedication to cultural preservation and his commitment to empowering artisans through education and technology.

With clarity and purpose, O'Brian presented the mentorship program to his team, outlining its objectives and envisioned impact. The program would pair artisans with mentors skilled in both traditional techniques and digital commerce, offering workshops, one-on-one sessions, and online resources. A key feature would be the creation of a digital platform within "Artisan Realms," dedicated to showcasing the artisans' journeys, from the mentorship process to the marketplace, thereby enriching the connection between artisans and the global community.

The team's response was overwhelmingly positive, their insights and enthusiasm further shaping the program. "This initiative," O'Brian declared, "embodies the spirit of 'Artisan Realms.' It's not just about preserving cultures but actively participating in their evolution. We're creating a legacy of empowerment, innovation, and interconnectedness."

This mentorship program, envisioned as a bridge between tradition and modernity, became a cornerstone of O'Brian's leadership. It was a testament to the enduring values instilled by his parents and his own vision for a future where "Artisan Realms" continued to thrive as a platform of cultural celebration, artisan empowerment, and global connection. In this way, O'Brian honored the past while crafting a legacy all his own, ensuring "Artisan Realms" remained a vibrant testament to the power of heritage, innovation, and shared humanity.

CHAPTER 44

SUPPORT SYSTEMS

As O'Brian navigated the complexities of leading "Artisan Realms" into the future, he encountered the formidable challenge of enhancing the platform with the already integrated Extended Reality (XR) technology. This endeavor, while exciting, brought to light the immense pressures of innovation and the need for a collaborative spirit within the team. During a period marked by technical challenges and the quest for groundbreaking solutions, O'Brian realized that true leadership was rooted in partnership, openness, and the collective strengths of his colleagues.

One evening, after a day fraught with hurdles related to the XR enhancement, O'Brian sat alone in his office. The vibrant glow of the cityscape outside his window did little to ease the sense of isolation he felt amidst the technological impasse. It was during this moment of reflection that Crystal, a young software engineer from the countryside who had been with the company for over three years, stepped into his office. Her arrival was unannounced, but her timing was impeccable.

"O'Brian," Crystal said, her tone both reassuring and earnest, "I've been thinking about the XR project. I believe there's a way through some of the obstacles we're facing. Maybe it's time we consider some unconventional approaches."

Crystal's background in software engineering, combined with her unique perspective from rural origins, had always given her a distinctive approach to problem-solving. Her suggestion sparked a glimmer of hope in O'Brian, a reminder that innovation often required stepping outside one's comfort zone and embracing diverse viewpoints.

Encouraged by Crystal's initiative, O'Brian convened a brainstorming session with his team, emphasizing collaboration and open dialogue. Crystal took the lead, outlining her ideas for enhancing the XR experience, suggesting innovative yet practical solutions that leveraged her deep understanding of both technology and user experience.

As the team engaged in vibrant discussions, inspired by Crystal's suggestions, it became evident that the path forward for the XR project would be paved with collective effort and creative thinking. Crystal's contributions were not just technical; they embodied the essence of "Artisan Realms" — bridging gaps, be they technological or cultural, through shared vision and teamwork.

In the subsequent weeks, O'Brian and the team, with Crystal playing a pivotal role, navigated the XR project's challenges with renewed vigor and creativity. They experimented with new technologies, integrated feedback from the artisan community, and iteratively refined the XR experience to ensure it was both immersive and authentic.

This period of intense development and collaboration brought the team closer, transforming "Artisan Realms" in ways that went beyond just technological advancements. The XR enhancement, once a daunting challenge, became a symbol of the platform's commitment to innovation, inclusivity, and the power of community.

Under O'Brian's leadership, and with Crystal's invaluable contributions, "Artisan Realms" not only succeeded in elevating the platform with XR but also reaffirmed the importance of collective wisdom and the strength found in diversity. This journey reinforced O'Brian's belief in his team and the legacy his parents left behind — a legacy of connection, culture, and collaboration that "Artisan Realms" would continue to build upon for the future.

CHAPTER 45

PERSONAL GROWTH

In the heart of a bustling "Artisan Realms," where innovation meets tradition, O'Brian stood as a beacon of youthful leadership. Yet, beneath the surface of his professional accomplishments, he grappled with the trials of inexperience —a journey of self-discovery, of finding his identity beyond the labels of CEO and prodigy.

One evening, after a day filled with meetings and decision-making, O'Brian found solace in the quiet of his favorite local café. It was here, amidst the soft murmur of conversations, with his only true friend and the gentle clatter of cups, that he allowed himself to just be O'Brian, not the CEO, not the genius, but a young man navigating the complexities of adulthood..

As he sipped his coffee, his thoughts drifted to a conversation he'd had with Mrs. Patel, who had become a confidant and mentor. "O'Brian," she had said, her voice warm and understanding, "it's okay to not have all the answers. You're doing an incredible job leading 'Artisan Realms,' but remember, you're also allowed to explore, to make mistakes, and to find out who you are outside of the company."

These words echoed in his mind, a comforting reminder that his worth wasn't solely tied to his achievements or the expectations placed upon him. O'Brian realized that part of his journey was to embrace the uncertainty of growing up, to explore his interests, passions, and the friendships - like this one, that offered glimpses of normalcy in his extraordinary life.

It was during his final university project, an unlikely partnership with a classmate who shared none of his entrepreneurial burdens, that O'Brian discovered a passion for music. Together, they delved into the world of melodies and harmonies, creating a soundtrack that spoke of their shared experiences, of hopes and dreams, and of the beauty in diversity.

This newfound interest in music became a vessel for O'Brian's personal growth. It taught him the value of collaboration, of listening not just to the notes but to the stories they told. Music became a language through which O'Brian could express himself, shedding the layers of CEO and prodigy to reveal the man beneath.

Amidst this exploration of this other side of himself, O'Brian also navigated the challenges of friendships and relationships. The dynamics of connecting with peers, of building bonds not defined by his professional identity, presented a labyrinth of emotional and social learning. He experienced the highs of companionship, the pangs of first love, and the inevitable heartbreaks, each moment a step toward understanding himself and others on a deeper level.

The unveiling of Version 2 of the XR feature at "Artisan Realms" was a momentous occasion, marking a significant leap forward in how users could connect with artisans and their crafts. At the press release, O'Brian, with a palpable sense of pride and excitement, introduced the innovative enhancements that defined the new version—faster navigation, enhanced image clarity, and a host of other technological advancements that promised a more immersive and seamless experience.

During his address, O'Brian made it a point to highlight Crystal's pivotal contribution to the project's success. "I want to take a moment to acknowledge someone without whom Version 2 of our XR feature wouldn't have been possible. Crystal, our brilliant software engineer, has been the driving force behind the innovations we're celebrating today. Her dedication, creativity, and innovative thinking have truly set a new standard for what we can achieve at 'Artisan Realms.'"

The acknowledgment brought a wave of applause from the audience, and Crystal, though bashful under the spotlight, felt a deep sense of accomplishment and pride.

Later that evening, O'Brian invited Crystal to a congratulatory dinner, a gesture of gratitude for her indispensable role in the project. As they dined in the soft glow of the restaurant's ambient lighting, the conversation flowed effortlessly, with Crystal taking the lead.

"I still can't believe I've come this far," Crystal began, her enthusiasm bubbling over. "Growing up in the countryside, I always dreamed of making an impact, of using technology to bridge gaps and bring people closer. But sitting in that press release today, seeing how far I've come... it's surreal."

O'Brian listened, captivated by her passion and the story of her journey. "It's incredible, Crystal. Your perspective, coming from a rural background and bringing that understanding to our urban-centric tech world, has been invaluable. It's exactly what 'Artisan Realms' needed."

Crystal laughed, a hint of shyness in her expression. "I remember my first day at 'Artisan Realms,' feeling like a fish out of water. But it's been such a journey of growth, not just professionally but personally too. I've learned so much from you, from the team, and from the artisans we work with. It's been... life-changing."

Throughout the dinner, O'Brian found himself increasingly drawn to Crystal, not just for her technical prowess but for her unique worldview and the simplicity with which she approached complex problems. Her passion for her work and her humble beginnings in the countryside added layers to her character that O'Brian found deeply intriguing.

As the evening came to a close, O'Brian escorted Crystal home, the night air cool and refreshing after the warmth of the restaurant. At her doorstep, he turned to her, gratitude shining in his eyes. "Crystal, thank you. For everything. Your work on Version 2 has been nothing short of extraordinary."

He gave her a hug, a gesture of thanks and recognition for her contributions. Crystal, still a bit shy under O'Brian's gaze, smiled. "Thank you, O'Brian. It's been an honor to be part of this journey. And tonight was just... really special."

As O'Brian drove away, the evening left him with a profound appreciation for Crystal, not just as a colleague but as someone whose passion, dedication, and humility had made a lasting impression on him and "Artisan Realms." The success of Version 2 was a shared achievement, but it was Crystal's spirit that had truly inspired him.

CHAPTER 46

FORGING AHEAD

In the vibrant morning light filtering through the windows of "Artisan Realms" headquarters, O'Brian, with a vision of innovation and growth, announced a significant promotion that marked a new chapter for the company. Amidst outlining future ventures and celebrating the team's achievements, he turned the spotlight on Crystal, acknowledging her pivotal role in the XR project's success and her innovative spirit.

"Before we proceed, I have an important announcement to make," O'Brian declared, his eyes finding Crystal in the room. "In recognition of her exceptional contributions and her visionary work on the XR project, I am promoting Crystal to the head of our engineering team."

The room erupted in applause, a chorus of congratulations directed at Crystal, who, though surprised, accepted the recognition with a mixture of pride and humility. O'Brian's confidence in her abilities was both an honor and a challenge, proof of her impact on "Artisan Realms."

Shortly after the meeting, as Crystal was basking in the glow of her new role, her long time friend Jacqueline came to visit. They were discussing plans for lunch when O'Brian happened by. Crystal introduced them, "This is my friend Jacqueline. We're about to head out for lunch."

"Pleasure to meet you, Jacqueline," O'Brian greeted warmly with a handshake that lingered just a little too long. "Did Crystal tell you about her promotion?"

Jacqueline, caught off guard, responded, "No, she didn't."

O'Brian chuckled, "It was literally five minutes ago, so I assume she wouldn't have had the chance." With a smile and a nod to Crystal, he added, "Nice meeting you, Jacqueline. I have another meeting to attend but I'll catch up with you later, Crystal."

As Crystal and Jacqueline headed to lunch, the conversation naturally veered towards O'Brian and Crystal's recent promotion. Jacqueline, intrigued by the dynamic young CEO, expressed her excitement and curiosity about Crystal's new role and the opportunities it presented.

"O'Brian seems to have a lot of faith in you," Jacqueline observed, sipping her coffee. "If he didn't believe in your abilities, he wouldn't have given you such a crucial position. You've proven time and again that you're more than capable of handling it."

Their lunch was a blend of personal catch-ups and professional discussions, with Crystal sharing her aspirations for the engineering team and the challenges she anticipated in her new role. Jacqueline, ever the supportive friend, reassured her, "You have a unique perspective and a knack for problem-solving that 'Artisan Realms' needs. You're going to excel in this position, just like you've excelled in everything else."

The conversation left Crystal feeling inspired and ready to embrace the challenges of her new role. O'Brian's decision to promote her was not just a recognition of her past contributions but also a vote of confidence in her ability to lead and innovate.

After their lunch outing, Crystal returned to the office, her spirits lifted by Jacqueline's support and the exciting prospects of her new role. As she moved through the corridors of "Artisan Realms," O'Brian caught up with her, his expression one of genuine enthusiasm.

"Crystal, about your promotion—let's celebrate it properly. Dinner on me," O'Brian suggested, his eyes twinkling with the idea of commemorating her achievement. "And why don't you bring Jacqueline along? She seems like an interesting person. Plus, I'd be keen to know more about her. Is she seeing anyone?"

Crystal felt a flutter of surprise at his inquiry, her mind grappling with the mixed emotions it evoked. Deep down, she harbored a subtle fondness for O'Brian, a sentiment complicated by their professional relationship and her own reservations. Nonetheless, she masked her internal conflict with a smile, eager to maintain the cheerful atmosphere.

"Sure, that sounds wonderful," Crystal replied, her voice steady despite the whirlwind of thoughts. "I'll invite Jacqueline. As for her dating life, it sounds like a perfect question for tonight."

The dinner was set at an upscale restaurant within one of Kingston's top five-star hotels, a venue that promised an evening of elegance and sophistication. As they gathered, the ambiance of the restaurant, with its cultured decor and soft lighting, set the stage for a memorable night.

Throughout the dinner, laughter and stories flowed freely. Jacqueline and Crystal shared anecdotes from their childhood, painting a picture of their enduring friendship for O'Brian. Intrigued by their tales, O'Brian found himself drawn into their world, his interest in Jacqueline growing with each shared memory.

Curiosity piqued, Jacqueline inquired about O'Brian's parents, having heard of their profound impact not just on "Artisan Realms" but on the broader community, including her family's bead-making business. O'Brian's response was heartfelt, reflecting his deep admiration and longing for his parents.

"My parents were extraordinary people," O'Brian shared, his voice tinged with both pride and nostalgia. "Working alongside them was a blessing. They instilled in me values and lessons that have shaped me into who I am today. Losing them was difficult, but I carry their legacy forward, trying to embody the principles they lived by."

The conversation, while touching on the absence of O'Brian's parents, also celebrated their lasting influence, not only on O'Brian but on those whose lives they had touched, like Jacqueline's family.

After the celebratory dinner, O'Brian, ever the gentleman, offered to drive Crystal and Jacqueline home. The evening had been filled with laughter, heartfelt stories, and a subtle undercurrent of new connections being formed. Crystal, with her mixed emotions carefully concealed, bid them goodnight as O'Brian first dropped her off at her doorstep. She felt a twinge of something indefinable as she watched the car drive away, a mix of happiness for the successful evening and a quiet contemplation of her feelings for O'Brian.

The drive to Jacqueline's home offered O'Brian and Jacqueline the opportunity to delve into more personal conversations, a chance to explore the initial spark of interest that had been kindled at dinner. They spoke candidly about their experiences with dating, their aspirations, and the curiosity they held for one another. The conversation flowed effortlessly, a sign of their mutual intrigue and the potential for something more. Before parting ways, they exchanged contact information, a promise of future conversations and explorations of the connection they both felt.

As O'Brian drove home, his mind was a whirlwind of thoughts — about the dinner, his growing interest in Jacqueline, and Crystal's invaluable role at "Artisan Realms." Yet looming large was the anticipation of next week's significant milestone: the company's 35th anniversary. This event was not just a celebration of "Artisan Realms'" longevity but also a testament to the legacy his parents had left behind and the future he was determined to forge.

The importance of the anniversary and the responsibility of delivering a speech that encapsulated the company's past achievements, present innovations, and future aspirations weighed on O'Brian. He understood that this speech was an opportunity to honor his parents' memory, rally his team, and inspire the "Artisan Realms" community towards continued growth and impact.

Arriving home, O'Brian dedicated the remainder of the night to preparing his speech. He sought to weave together the rice mural of "Artisan Realms'" history with the vision that had guided its founders and the innovations that promised to propel it into the future. As he reflected on the journey of "Artisan Realms," from its humble beginnings to its current stature as a global platform connecting artisans with a worldwide audience, O'Brian felt a deep connection to his parents' dreams and a renewed commitment to leading the company in a way that honored their legacy while embracing the challenges and opportunities of the modern world.

CHAPTER 47

REMEMBERING THE PAST, BUILDING THE FUTURE

As the grand anniversary ball of "Artisan Realms" drew near, O'Brian, carrying the weight of his parents' legacy and the anticipation of the future, made a decision that would add a personal twist to the evening. He invited Jacqueline as his plus one to the event, seizing the opportunity to deepen the budding connection they had discovered in their recent conversations. This decision, made amidst the whirl of preparations and reflections, symbolized a step forward—not just for "Artisan Realms" but for O'Brian personally, as he opened himself up to new relationships and experiences.

The gala, a vibrant celebration of "Artisan Realms'" journey and its community, was held in a beautifully restored hall that echoed the platform's ethos of blending tradition with innovation. As guests arrived, the air buzzed with excitement and the shared anticipation of commemorating such a significant milestone. Artisans from diverse backgrounds, team members, and supporters mingled, their conversations an array of stories that "Artisan Realms" had helped weave together.

Crystal, among the attendees, experienced a whirlwind of emotions. She felt a profound sense of pride in the company's achievements and the role she had played in its success, especially with the recent launch of Version 2 of the XR feature. Yet, witnessing O'Brian and Jacqueline together stirred complex feelings within her. The happiness she felt for her friend's joy was tinged with a hint of sadness, a reflection of her unspoken affection for O'Brian. The evening, with its celebrations and acknowledgments, was a bittersweet experience for Crystal, who couldn't help but wonder what might have been had she acted on those initial feelings.

Throughout the night, O'Brian, with Jacqueline by his side, engaged with guests, sharing stories of "Artisan Realms'" past and visions for its future. The highlight came when O'Brian took the stage, his speech a heartfelt tribute to his parents, Jason and Kimberly, and a declaration of the ambitious path he envisioned for "Artisan Realms." He spoke of sustainability, community empowerment, and the launch of new initiatives designed to expand the platform's impact and reach.

Jacqueline, intrigued by O'Brian's dedication and the legacy of his parents, found herself drawn even more to the young CEO. Their conversations throughout the evening revealed shared values and aspirations, laying the groundwork for a deeper relationship. O'Brian, too, felt a growing connection to Jacqueline, appreciating her curiosity about his work and her genuine interest in the mission of "Artisan Realms."

As the evening wound down, the ball had not only celebrated the company's 35th anniversary but also marked the beginning of new chapters for those within the "Artisan Realms" community. For O'Brian, it was a reaffirmation of his commitment to his parents' vision and the future of the platform. For Crystal, it was a night of mixed emotions, a reminder of the paths not taken and the hope for what lay ahead.

Jacqueline's feelings were a mix of excitement and caution as the anniversary ball came to a close. While she was genuinely happy and intrigued by the connection she felt with O'Brian, her past experiences in relationships cast a shadow of reservation over her.. The night had been magical, filled with stories of innovation, culture, and community that resonated deeply with her values. Yet, as she stepped into the possibility of exploring a relationship with O'Brian, she couldn't shake off the apprehension borne from her previous heartaches.

In a quiet moment, as they stepped away from the remaining guests, Jacqueline found the courage to open up to O'Brian about her hesitations. Under the soft glow of the venue's lights, she shared her past struggles, explaining how they had shaped her approach to new relationships. "I'm really happy about tonight, and I feel there's something special here," she admitted, her voice laced with a vulnerability she rarely showed. "But my last relationship left me quite wary. I just don't want to rush into anything and make the same mistakes."

O'Brian listened intently, his expression one of understanding and compassion. He recognized the significance of her sharing such personal feelings with him, and he felt a deep respect for her honesty. "Jacqueline," he responded gently, his eyes meeting hers, "I understand, and I really appreciate you being so open with me. I've had my share of challenges too, and I know how important it is to take things at a pace that feels right for both of us."

He paused for a moment, choosing his words with care. "I'm here, and I'm interested in getting to know you better, at whatever pace you're comfortable with. Open communication is key for me, and I believe that as long as we're honest about our feelings and expectations, we can navigate this together."

Jacqueline felt a weight lift off her shoulders, reassured by O'Brian's empathy and willingness to take things slow. His response not only showed his understanding but also his commitment to building something based on mutual respect and open dialogue. It was a refreshing change from her past experiences, offering a glimpse of hope that this time could be different.

As they parted ways that evening, with promises to talk and spend more time together, both Jacqueline and O'Brian felt a cautious optimism about the future. For Jacqueline, the evening had transformed from a celebration of "Artisan Realms" to the beginning of a new, personal journey—one that she was now more open to exploring, thanks to O'Brian's supportive and patient approach. For O'Brian, the night had reaffirmed his belief in the power of communication and connection, not just within the realm of his business but in the realm of personal relationships as well.

The anniversary ball, thus, became a pivotal point not only for "Artisan Realms" but also for O'Brian and Jacqueline, marking the start of a journey of discovery, understanding, and, hopefully, deepening connection.

CHAPTER 48

CHALLENGES OF LEADERSHIP

As O'Brian's journey as CEO of "Artisan Realms" unfolded, the initial thrill of leading his parents' creation into innovative directions was tempered by the sobering responsibilities of his role. Leadership meant navigating the delicate balance between growth and integrity, making decisions that resonated with the core ethos of "Artisan Realms" while confronting the practical challenges of running a business.

During a critical period for the company, a strategy meeting brought O'Brian face to face with a dilemma that would test the very foundation of "Artisan Realms." A proposal from a globally recognized corporation presented a tempting path to financial prosperity and broader market reach. However, this opportunity came laced with compromises that threatened to dilute the ethical and artisan-centric values that defined "Artisan Realms."

The discussion within the senior team was charged with tension, as the potential benefits of the deal were weighed against its ethical implications. O'Brian, absorbing the diverse viewpoints, felt the weight of his parents' legacy as a guiding force in his decision-making process.

Acknowledging the potential gains, O'Brian voiced his concerns, "The advantages of this partnership are clear, yet we must ask ourselves at what cost. Are we willing to betray the trust of our artisans and the ethical stance we've proudly and publicly upheld?"

O'Brian's intervention shifted the discussion towards a deeper reflection on Artisan Realms' mission and long-term vision. The decision before them wasn't just a business calculation; it was a moral crossroads that would define the company's identity moving forward.

That night, O'Brian sat on the roof of the office building, gazing at the Kingston city skyline and stars, pondering what to do. Crystal, working late, noticed him taking the emergency exit to the roof. Worried, she followed him up.

"What's going on with the deal?" she asked, approaching him.

He replied, "I know what to do, but am I doing the right thing? I want to respect my parents' wishes but also ensure the legacy of Artisan Realms lives on."

Crystal listened intently and then said, "You want to know what I would do? I would reject the offer and keep nurturing the platform into the powerhouse it's meant to be."

O'Brian smiled, "That's what I was thinking too." Shaking his head, he added, "As always, you know exactly what to say. I'm so glad I have you in my life." He got up, hugged her, and said, "Thank you."

The following morning, O'Brian decided to reject the corporate partnership. This bold move sent ripples through the business community and Artisan Realms itself, reaffirming the company's dedication to its founding principles and echoing the integrity and vision of Jason and Kimberly.

The aftermath of this decision was complex. While some stakeholders expressed concern and even opposition, a wave of support emerged from those who shared "Artisan Realms'" commitment to ethical entrepreneurship. The artisans at the heart of the platform and a segment of the consumer base rallied around O'Brian's decision, appreciating the company's unwavering commitment to its values.

In the wake of this pivotal moment, O'Brian, bolstered by the support of his team and the broader "Artisan Realms" community, embarked on a mission to explore new avenues for growth. These efforts were grounded in the company's ethos, focusing on partnerships and initiatives that offered sustainable expansion without compromising on the ethical standards that were its hallmark.

This chapter in O'Brian's leadership was a revelation of the enduring influence of his parents' values and his own resolve to navigate the challenges of modern entrepreneurship with integrity. It underscored the complexity of leading "Artisan Realms" in a way that honored its past while courageously charting a path forward, guided by the principles of ethical practice, community support, and cultural preservation.

CHAPTER 49

LEGACY REALIZED

In this pivotal moment of reflection and celebration, O'Brian also took the opportunity to acknowledge his recent engagement to Jacqueline, an event that symbolized not just personal joy but the unwavering support and partnership they had cultivated over the years. "And tonight, I'm also celebrating something very personal," O'Brian shared, his voice warm with the joy of shared commitment. "My proposal to Jacqueline, who has been by my side with her unwavering support. Her belief in me and in 'Artisan Realms' has been a source of strength."

Their happiness was palpable, resonating through the crowd as they cheered, applauding not just for the success of "Artisan Realms" but for the personal milestones that intertwined with the company's journey.

However, amidst the laughter and the clinking of glasses, O'Brian's thoughts momentarily drifted to Crystal, a key architect of "Artisan Realms'" growth and a dear friend. Leaning closer to Jacqueline, he whispered, "Has anyone seen Crystal tonight?" His voice was laced with concern, showing the depth of his respect and affection for Crystal. "I know she's on a hiatus, but I sent her an invitation. It saddens me that she might not be here to share in this moment."

Jacqueline nodded, understanding the significance of Crystal's absence in the celebration. The question lingered between them, a shared hope for her presence.

As if summoned by their conversation, Crystal appeared, her arrival filling the gap in the evening's joy. O'Brian, relieved and delighted, approached her with a genuine smile. "Crystal, you made it! I was hoping you'd be here. Are you okay?" His concern echoed the years of friendship and collaboration, highlighting the special place Crystal held in the "Artisan Realms" story and in his heart.

Crystal's presence brought a sense of completeness to the celebration, her contributions to "Artisan Realms" and her support of O'Brian and Jacqueline cherished by all. "I wouldn't miss this, O'Brian. Seeing everything you've achieved, the way you've grown—it's incredible. I'm so happy for you both," she said, her words reflecting the deep bonds forged through shared dreams and challenges.

The evening continued with a spirit of unity and joy, as the "Artisan Realms" community celebrated not only the platform's milestones and O'Brian's personal happiness but also the enduring connections that had sustained them. Crystal's presence underscored the collective achievements and the individual journeys that intertwined within the vibrant mix of "Artisan Realms." In this gathering of friends, colleagues, and partners, the essence of "Artisan Realms"—built on community, innovation, and ethical integrity—shone brightly, a beacon of what can be accomplished when shared values guide the way.

CHAPTER 50

LEGACY AND NEW BEGINNINGS

As the sun dipped below the horizon, casting a serene glow over the "Artisan Realms" headquarters, O'Brian stood amidst the tranquility of the rooftop garden, contemplating the profound journey that had led him to this pivotal moment. It was here, in this oasis of calm and reflection, that he wrestled with the decision to step away from the daily operations of the company he had nurtured in the legacy of his parents, Jason and Kimberly. This decision was not born from a desire to distance himself from "Artisan Realms," but rather a commitment to embrace a new chapter in his life with his fiancée Jacqueline and their unborn child.

Before O'Brian could share his decision with the world, he met up with the Patels for coffee, ready to share his big news. "I'm going to step down as CEO," he told them. "I'll still be on the board of directors, but I need to focus on my family right now. I'll be there to help in the background, but I won't have a major role in the company for now."

Mr. Patel nodded, not surprised but understanding. "You've done a wonderful job filling your parents' shoes and exceeding all expectations," he said.

Mrs. Patel chimed in, "So, who will be the new CEO?"

O'Brian replied, "I was thinking about Crystal. She might resist at first because of her loyalty to me, but I believe she's more than capable."

Mr. Patel agreed. "Yes, she is more than capable. She has shown resilience, brilliance, and leadership. She'll make a fine CEO and has the respect required for the role."

Mrs. Patel asked, "When do you plan on telling her?"

"Today, if possible," O'Brian responded.

Mr. Patel smiled. "I'm so proud of you and all that you've accomplished. Your parents would be so happy to see the man you've become."

With the support of the Patels, O'Brian sought out Crystal, a friend and confidant whose brilliance and dedication had been instrumental in the growth of "Artisan Realms." Pulling her aside, he entrusted her with his intent to step down as CEO and asked her to take up the mantle in his stead.

Crystal, taken aback by the suddenness of the request, initially resisted. "No, you can't leave," she protested, her voice a mixture of surprise and concern. "I know I'm capable of supporting you while you run the company, but I don't know if I can do it on my own."

O'Brian, with a reassuring calmness, responded, "Crystal, you can run this company and two more with the power of your brain and vigor. Trust me, I've thought about this deeply."

After a moment of contemplation, weighed down by the enormity of the responsibility yet buoyed by O'Brian's faith in her, Crystal acquiesced. "OK, I'll do it, but only if you'll be there to support me when I need you most, whenever that time comes."

O'Brian's response was immediate and heartfelt. With a smile, he extended his hands, lifting her in a reassuring hug. "Yes, I'll always be here. Just call me," he promised.

Crystal, now smiling through her apprehension, sought one more assurance. "You promise?"

"I promise," O'Brian affirmed, sealing the new chapter for "Artisan Realms" with a pledge of unwavering support.

This moment marked a significant transition, not just for O'Brian and Crystal, but for "Artisan Realms" as a whole. As the announcement of O'Brian's decision to step away and appoint Crystal as his successor was made, the community that had grown around "Artisan Realms" reacted with a mixture of surprise and support. The send-off party for O'Brian, attended by friends, and colleagues, was a testament to the impact O'Brian had made and the bright future that lay ahead under Crystal's leadership.

"Your parents would be so proud of you," Mr. Patel assured O'Brian, his words echoing the sentiment of all who had gathered. "You've achieved so much on their behalf."

This transition was more than a change in leadership; it was a reaffirmation of "Artisan Realms'" values and a commitment to its future. O'Brian's choice to prioritize his family, entrusting Crystal with the company, was a decision made in the spirit of the legacy left by Jason and Kimberly—a legacy of innovation, culture, and community.

As O'Brian embarks on this new chapter of his life, his heart is full, knowing that "Artisan Realms" remains in capable hands. Crystal, bolstered by O'Brian's trust and the support of the "Artisan Realms" community, steps into her role with determination and vision. Together, they stand on the threshold of a future filled with endless possibilities, guided by the enduring impact of love, family, and the pursuit of a life that balances personal fulfillment with professional achievement. The story of "Artisan Realms" continues, its narrative enriched by the contributions of its founders, its stewards, and the vibrant community it serves—a living testament to the belief that business can indeed be a force for positive change, celebrating the human spirit and bridging worlds.

LEGAL NOTICES

the contents of this publication. Any reliance you place on such information is therefore strictly at your own risk.

Governing Law: This publication and any dispute arising out of its use are governed by the laws of Jamaica, without regard to its conflict of law provisions.

Limitation of Liability: The author and publisher shall not be liable for any direct, indirect, incidental, consequential, or punitive damages arising out of or in connection with the use of this publication.

For Permission Requests: Requests for permission to reproduce any part of this publication should be addressed to the publisher, directed to "Attention: Permissions Coordinator," at the following email address: odecebrooks@gmail.com

ACKNOWLEDGMENTS

Completing this novel has been a journey that stretched far beyond my imagination, and it would not have been possible without the support, patience, and love of many incredible individuals.

First and foremost, I wish to express my deepest gratitude to my family, who have been my rock throughout this process.

Editorial Team
Daneil Hodges
Odece Brooks

I am immensely thankful to my editor, Daneil Hodges, whose keen eye and sage advice transformed my manuscript into the polished novel it is today. Your guidance was invaluable.

Special Thanks
A special thanks to, those who believed in this story from its inception and have been a guiding light throughout its development.

Lastly, I want to acknowledge you, the reader. Thank you for giving my words a place in your world. I hope this story resonates with you, as much as it has with me.

ABOUT THE AUTHOR

Odece Brooks, a passionate young Jamaican, found his heart deeply intertwined with the vibrant soul of his country. Infused with love for Jamaica and technology, this book reflects the rich cultural heritage of Jamaica, seamlessly blended with the advancements of modern technology.

Raised in Kingston and parts of Manchester, Odece's upbringing profoundly influences his storytelling. Immersed in an environment rich with cultural traditions and values, he developed a deep appreciation for his heritage. In his writing, Odece skillfully weaves together fiction and reality, creating narratives that captivate and inspire. His stories celebrate the beauty and resilience of Jamaican culture, brought to life with imaginative elements that spark wonder and curiosity.

With a vision to connect the world through storytelling and digital experiences, Odece continues to inspire and lead with his unique perspective and unwavering commitment to his roots.

Scan Me

www.ingramcontent.com/pod-product-compliance
Lightning Source LLC
Chambersburg PA
CBHW060649260626
47161CB00008B/3060